JOSHUA'S COUNTRY

ALSO BY GERARD DE MARIGNY

What readers are saying of …
THE WATCHMAN OF EPHRAIM (Cris De Niro, Book 1)

"For a real page-turning thriller with twists and one which keeps the reader hooked, read this book."
beckvalleybooks

"The Watchman of Ephraim was a ride. I loved every minute I spent with the story and characters. I found myself getting choked up with the description of the events of 9/11. I was totally drawn into the story and couldn't put the book down."
Daniel N. Wallace

"Just finished reading The Watchman of Ephraim and I must give a very enthusiastic WOW! Gerard de Marigny has crafted a very exciting and engrossing story of international espionage with vibrant, fully-developed characters who the reader connects with. Throw in a few exotic locales and you have a totally worthy successor to either James Bond or Jack Ryan. Read it – you won't be disappointed."
Musicman

What readers are saying of …
SIGNS OF WAR (Cris De Niro, Book 2)

"An action-packed, patriotic read that held me interest from start to finish."
Francie VW

"The part that I loved most about this book, as well as this series, is that the author has taken the time to research the military, the government, the weapons, the many different locations, technology, etc."
James Mathis

"Heart-stopping action, impossible decisions, a touch of romance, suspense, betrayal and courage set the tone for this thrilling installment in the Cris De Niro series. Gerard de Marigny writes with flair and attention to detail, ensnaring the reader in his web from the first page. If you enjoy political thrillers jam-packed with action and extraordinary characters, you won't want to miss Signs of War!"
Wendy L. Hines "MindSpot"

What readers are saying of …
PROJECT 111 (Cris De Niro, Book 4)

"Another home run on a well-executed story that has plenty of suspense, action, thrilling moments. The story unfolds in a well-paced storyline that at the end, you are left wanting the story to continue. I am a big fan of de Marigny novels and look forward for more to come."
Robert "Robear" (Amazon Review)

"If you enjoy Thor, Flynn, Siva, Coes, or any books in this genre, you'll love this series! The depth of the characters is so well done you get hooked from the first page on. I'd recommend reading the books in order. Not that they don't stand on their own, they do, but the way the author builds upon each character really engages you in their lives. Love the patriotism, attention to detail and storylines. Keep 'em coming!!!"
Barb (Amazon Review)

"This book was a delight to read … The development of the main characters is great and believable. I like how everyone that is connected to Cris becomes family to him, even the Russian prisoner. I enjoyed the little bits of humor every now and then … I like how the author references actual events that happened in the real world in this book … This was a great book."
Bobmandingo (Amazon Review)

What readers are saying of ...
NOTHING SO GLORIOUS (Cris De Niro, Book 5)

"I have read every book in the Cris De Niro series. Nothing So Glorious not only delivers, it takes this series to new heights. Once again Gerard mixes today's headlines with a story line that keeps you on the edge of your seat. One of the best features of these books are the characters. You feel you know them and you feel their pain when one of the group is injured or in harm's way. Get to know Cris, Mugsy, Michelle, Johnny F. and the man in black. Once you meet them, you will never forget them."
Bob Freidel

"Have truly enjoyed this series and the character development. Gerard is an excellent story teller, who creates suspense and action that makes it hard to put these books down. Have read the 5-book series in less than 10 days. Cannot wait for the next one."
Lon E Frye

"Author writer Gerard de Marigny has once again astounded me with his latest work. The only downside is that I have to wait for the next installment of the next Cris De Niro book. It is only an amount of time before this series becomes the next big Hollywood franchise. I can't wait for these stories to become larger than life on the big screen. It's inevitable. Great writing by a great author/storyteller."
Michael Gerbino

What readers are saying of …
NEW DETROIT (Cris De Niro, Book 6)

"Gerard de Marigny is a Master Thrill writer! New Detroit, as all his other works, is filled with heart-stopping, breath-holding, mind-blowing action, sometimes all at once! The characters are real people. Their actions and reactions right on the spot. The scenes are so vivid, close your eyes and you can see it. You feel the determination of Cris De Niro and his cohorts and you feel the aggravation of surrounding people turn to terror. I cannot wait for his next book, WHITE WIDOW (ARCHANGEL, Mission Logs 3).
Jody McLee

JOSHUA'S COUNTRY

GERARD DE MARIGNY

JarRyJorNo Publishing

HENDERSON

JarRyJorNo
Publishing

Published by JarRyJorNo Publishing
Henderson, Nevada

Edited by Lisa de Marigny

ISBN: 1794682600
ISBN-13: 978-1794682603

Library of Congress Control Number: 2017916737

1 3 5 9 10 8 6 4 2

In memory of the victims of the Route 91 Harvest Festival massacre in Las Vegas, Nevada, on Sunday evening, 01 October, 2017.

Prayers continue for the families of those who lost their lives, and for the victims that lived through the assault, but who are still facing many more health struggles, including Rylie Golgart, the daughter of a dear friend of my wife and mine. #VegasStrong

(Gerard de Marigny)

AUTHOR'S NOTE

Originally, I wrote Joshua's Country with one simple concept in mind; one simple question to be answered: What would happen if the ideological hatred of an Islamic extremist encountered an old cantankerous cowboy?

Yet, *Joshua's Country* became less a war story or terrorist tale than a story of a man's disillusionment with his country and dysfunctional relationship with his family. Joshua was a prideful man who paid a painful price for that pride.

In the end, *Joshua's Country* is a story of second chances ... and the power of love when the family is united.

"The strength of a family, like the strength of an army, is in its loyalty to each other."--Mario Puzo

Joshua's Country is my first published story outside the CRIS DE NIRO universe. I am forever grateful to God Almighty for filling my heart and mind with great stories to tell, and endowing me with the ability to tell them.

Eternal thanks to my wife Lisa and sons Jared, Ryan, Jordan, and Noah. Your faith and support are my greatest blessings.

Very special thanks and everlasting gratitude to my mentor, writing partner, and amigo-for-life, legendary producer Mike Greenburg. Our time is now, bro!!

Continued thanks to my ever-growing group of friends on my website, Twitter, Goodreads, Facebook, and LinkedIn … I'm very grateful for your friendship and support!

And a personal note to all the readers of my stories - I consider it the highest honor to entertain you. I deeply appreciate your giving me that opportunity and pray you will allow me to entertain you for many years to come!

All my hopes … All praise to Him!
g

JOSHUA'S COUNTRY

CHAPTER 1

THE DOUBLE-J RANCH
PECOS COUNTY, TEXAS
MORNING

The leather-faced cowboy stood with his hands tucked into his back pockets. Donning a well-worn white felt cowboy hat slightly tilted back on his head, white shirt with pearl snaps, dust-covered Wranglers, and scuffed boots, he scanned the landscape with dark, deep-set eyes.

Cattle dotted the grassy countryside to the east as far as the eye could see. To the west, the spire of an oil derrick rose up on the horizon into the bright blue sky. In between, the prairie stretched out to a band of rolling hills, its rich green grass bespeckled with a patchwork of feed grain crops.

The cowboy nodded his head with a touch of melancholy, until his gaze was broken by a gentle gust of wind that brought an antique glass wind chime to life behind him. He turned toward the sound. The chime was perched over a simple headstone that read, "Sarah Jacobs, 1952 – 2012, Beloved wife, mother, grandmother."

The tinkling of the dainty instrument brought back fond memories, and for a moment, a soft smile added a few more wrinkles to the cowboy's weathered face. Joshua Jacobs' smile grew, but his melancholy remained. The chimes were his wife's favorite.

In each house they had ever lived, the old Chinese wind chime used to hang at one end of the porch. Memories of sitting with Sarah watching the sun set, while listening to the melodies of the wind filled his mind.

He recalled how Sarah would lay her head on his lap and fall asleep. Then, when James was born he would stroke her hair while she nursed the infant. Sarah would put words to the airy lullaby. Her voice was as soothing to him as it was to their baby.

Joshua's smile melted away as he thought of James. The memories made him look over at his son's headstone set next to Sarah's. His eyes filled with tears.

James's headstone was identical to Sarah's except for two things: a triangular enclosure built into the stone with a Plexiglas front that housed the flag Joshua was handed at James's funeral, and a five-inch oval shaped frame located at the top of the triangle that housed a photo of James in his dress blues. Under the triangle, the inscription read, "Major James Lee Jacobs, USMC, 1970 – 2015, Beloved husband, son, and father."

Joshua turned his back on the graves and looked in the direction of a white pickup truck heading towards him across the grass-covered range. He let his eyes gaze beyond the pickup to the two stately haciendas in the distance.

Located one hundred yards apart, one was the home he and Sarah built and lived in until her death. Joshua still lived there, but since Sarah's death he slept in one of the guest rooms. The other was supposed to be a wedding present from Joshua and Sarah to his son James and his wife, Katy. Instead, it sat vacant for the last 23 years.

Staring at the majestic structure, Joshua recalled the argument he had with his son at James's wedding that led to the house standing vacant.

"James, you're married now. It's time for you to quit the Corps and come back to work on the ranch."

I never wanted him to join the damn Marines in the first place! He said he wanted to follow in my footsteps. I told him if I had to do it over again, I wouldn't have joined the Corps, but he wouldn't buy it.

Our arguments still haunt me. Raised voices led to regretful words. Sarah and Katy were upset with us, but we paid them no mind. Then I gave him that damn ultimatum … the Corps or the ranch. I wasn't gonna wait for him to assume his role here any longer. I figured the spread I built for them would be just the kicker to get him to give in.

But he was more like me than I knew.

He told me where I could stick the house and the ranch. He wasn't gonna leave the Corps.

Joshua sighed deeply.

A man's gotta do what a man's gotta do.

I respected that much about his decision. I wonder if he felt the same way about mine ….

The pickup ground to a halt in front of him and a tall old African-American man stepped out. He was wearing a similar snap-buttoned shirt, Wranglers, and scuffed boots, but on his head, cocked at an angle, was a sweat-soaked baseball cap with the ranch's "Double-J" brand emblazed on it.

Rufus Pepper had been a friend of Joshua's since Parris Island 1964. Joshua belonged to Platoon 291, Second Recruit Battalion, and Pepper, then Sgt. Pepper, was the platoon's drill instructor.

It wasn't until three years later when the song and album came out, that Pepper started getting razzed with lyrics from the Beatles' famous song. Joshua even bought Pepper a "Sgt. Pepper's Lonely

Hearts Club Band" T-shirt while on liberty, had it gift-wrapped and sent to him. Pepper never wore the shirt, but he kept it. Something about Joshua made him keep it. He "liked the cut of his jib," an old jarhead phrase, taken from 17th century pirates.

It was unusual for drill instructors and recruits to maintain communication after basic training. It was even more unusual for a DI and a recruit to become friends, but Joshua and Pepper discovered they had deeper roots. They were both born and raised in the same part of West Texas, just a town over from one another, although there was a nine-year age difference between them.

When Joshua shipped out in 1968, he went back home to become a rancher, as his dad and granddad had been. It took him seven years to work his way up to foreman. By that time, he and Sarah had saved enough to purchase the first patch of land that eventually became the Double-J.

Joshua knew he was going to need a foreman, so he reached out to Sgt. Pepper, who by that time had already put in his twenty. He knew Pepper couldn't remain a DI forever and was intending to return home anyway, so it was mutually beneficial.

By the time James got married, the Double-J had grown into one of the largest diversified ranches in the state of Texas, which meant the world. Starting with cattle, Joshua purchased more land to plant feed grain crops. Once again, he reached out to a former Marine buddy who served with him in Lima Company of the "3/3," 3rd battalion 3rd Marines, Alfredo "Freddie" Gonzalez. Freddie grew up just miles away from the ranch, on the Mexican side of the border. There he was raised to be a farmer, as was his father and grandfather before him.

At the same time, on a hunch and a tip from a friend, Joshua had purchased the mineral rights to a tract of land adjacent to the land he intended for farming. For over one-hundred years that land had operated as a working cattle ranch, but the owner had died.

Snake Vela, another member of Lima Company who coincidentally joined the Corps with Joshua was the foreman on that ranch. Snake told Joshua that, before the owner died, he confided that there were signs of oil on the land. Snake couldn't afford to purchase the mineral rights on his own, so he pleaded with Joshua to purchase them. Joshua agreed under one condition, if oil was found, Snake would be in charge of the operation. That meant that Snake would have to hone up on hydrocarbon mining. Joshua knew that Snake was a fast learner in anything he put his mind to.

Snake was a full-blooded Lipan Apache whose family had migrated west from McAllen, Texas when he was just a boy. He grew up in a shack not far from the grade school Joshua attended.

Snake and Joshua first met when a football hit Joshua in the face on his walk home from school. Snake had thrown it, but the ball belonged to a friend of Snake's who knew young Joshua as a bit of a bully. Snake's friend ran as soon as he saw the ball hit Joshua's face, but Snake decided to retrieve it. A fight ensued that, to this day, both say they won, although both agree that the fight marked the beginning of their friendship.

As soon as he graduated high school, Joshua dragged his mother down to the Marine recruiting office to allow him to sign up, since seventeen-year-olds needed parental permission. On the way, Snake saw them and decided to tag along. By the time they arrived, Joshua had convinced Snake to join with him. Snake's parents had both died the year before, so even though she wasn't his legal guardian, Joshua's mother figured a way to give permission for Snake too.

Upon completing basic training, Joshua asked Sgt. Pepper if he could keep Snake and him together. After Pepper chewed his ass out with, "Marines go where they're sent …," Joshua was pleased to find that he and Snake were transferred to Lima Company, third-third. Pepper told them later that the least he could do for two of Texas's favorite sons were to let them die next to each other on the field of battle.

Within ten years of purchasing the mineral rights, oil was indeed discovered, which allowed Joshua to purchase all the land west of his ranch. That's when the Double-J ranch became a solid block comprised of 198,000 acres (28 miles east to west & 14 miles north to south). Joshua gave Pepper, Snake, and Freddie an equity interest in the ranch, along with spreads of their own, located on the Double-J.

Pepper didn't have any living relatives, but Snake and Freddie did. Eventually, they both relocated their extended families to their spreads. Pepper called Snake's spread, "The Nation," and Freddie's spread, "Lil' Mexico." Neither man was offended. After all, Joshua made the three of them very wealthy, though—as Joshua would declaim—"you'd never know it from their work ethic."

The truth was they all worked just as hard as they had when they started out together. The only difference was Pepper, Freddie, and Snake expressed their joy from their success. Joshua showed none, not since James died, except rare times when his grandson was with him.

Other than the cattle, grazing land, feed crops, and minerals, the ranch was teeming with wildlife including deer, elk, antelope, javelin, wild turkey, bobcats, coyotes, doves, and quail. The job of managing the wildlife was turned over to Joshua's daughter-in-law, Katy. Just graduated from veterinary school, she was the natural choice, though she had to be convinced to take the job by Pepper. He told her Joshua needed her around, even though he never expressed it.

Although James and Joshua had never rekindled their relationship, Katy had remained close with Sarah until her death. As for her relationship with Joshua, she considered him akin to a black bear. She was fine with him as long as she didn't have to be in his company for too long, because like a black bear, her father-in-law was unpredictable. From afar, he seemed harmless enough, but get too close and he may slap the ground, huff and blow, and chomp his teeth to get you to move to a comfortable distance away.

When Pepper offered her the job, Katy accepted it under the condition that she didn't have to report to Joshua. Pepper knew Joshua would be fine with that. He knew he loved his daughter-in-law, just like he loved James.

While James's relationship with Joshua was cold and Katy's relationship with Joshua was distant, that wasn't true of their son, Joshua Jacobs II. Young Josh was named after his grandpa, even though James and Joshua weren't getting along at the time of his birth. It had nothing to do with friendship or love. It had to do with respect. Even though James couldn't get along with his dad, he always respected him.

Despite the "old man's" ill-temperament, young Josh loved his grandfather. James and Katy allowed their son's relationship to flourish with Joshua. Young Josh looked up to his grandfather, and to Joshua, young Josh was the apple of his eye, though he rarely showed it beyond the look of pride he couldn't conceal. There was always a special connection between them.

While James was away on one tour of duty or the next, Joshua taught young Jake everything he knew – how to hunt and fish, raise cattle, and run the ranch. In time, Joshua hoped that his grandson would move into the house he built for James and Katy and eventually take over when he passed on, but he also knew the young man would have to make up his own mind, like his dad had before him.

The absence of a promise did not stop Joshua from changing his will to make young Josh the heir to all he owned. Old Joshua was crushed, when like his dad, at seventeen, young Josh decided to join the Marines.

Joshua wanted so badly to try and talk Josh out of it, but he remembered how that worked against him with James. He wouldn't risk alienating his grandson. Instead, he prayed every night that someday Josh would return to the ranch.

The strain of losing Sarah and James and the subsequent absence of young Josh in his life, darkened Joshua even more. It had gotten to the point that he almost never left the ranch, and other than Pepper, Snake, and Freddie, Joshua rarely interacted with another person. Even with them he was cantankerous, but the three understood. Twice they stood with him and cried the tears he could not cry, at Sarah and James's funerals.

Yet, it seemed that the effect of their deaths hadn't wounded his heart as much as the day young Josh left for Parris Island. Five years had passed. With each year, the three watched as Joshua visibly grew older, more tired, and bad tempered.

Pepper approached with his arms crossed. He knew what he was in for.

Joshua snarled, "I thought I told you never to bother me here?"

Pepper flashed a sarcastic grin, "If you carried your phone with you, I wouldn't have had to come out here, at all."

Joshua turned to face the grave stones. He realized the wind chime stopped its music. He took a deep breath, "What's up?"

"Snake's grandson just came home."

"Benigno finished vet school, did he?"

"He did indeed, thanks to Katy's tutoring."

Joshua turned sharply at the mention of his daughter-in-law's name, "Benny was always a smart kid. He would've done just fine on his own."

Joshua walked past him and headed for the passenger side of the pickup. He spoke over his shoulder, "Is that all you came out here to tell me?"

Pepper raised a brow and followed after him, not replying until he got behind the wheel, "Snake and his family are having a pow-wow later at his house. He asked me to ask you if you'd come."

Joshua never turned his head. He just stared out the windshield, "All them Apaches all whiskeyed up ... hell no."

Pepper flashed a knowing grin, "Snake figured you'd say that, so he told me to take you over there now. At least let Benny show you his diploma."

Joshua rubbed his forehead and nodded in reply.

Pepper turned the key in the ignition and revved the motor before putting the pickup in gear, "But first, we gotta head over to Lil Mexico. Freddie's grandniece just showed up on his doorstep with her husband in tow and a baby in her belly. She's nine months pregnant and ready to drop any time now."

Joshua punched the dashboard, "Damn it if I didn't tell Freddie a hundred times—"

Pepper mouthed it with him, "No illegals on the Double-J!"

Pepper continued, "He knows that, Joshua. He didn't invite them. They just showed up."

"How the hell they get past Snake's Apache warriors at the gate? They're supposed to be our ranch's security. Some damn security ... can't even spot a nine-month pregnant wetback and her baby-daddy."

Pepper slammed the brakes, "Joshua Jacobs … you're a nasty, mean old bear with a thorn stuck in your paw … but one thing you ain't is a bigot! Our security spotted Carmen and Rito—their names, by the way—the moment they approached the Double-J's main gates. They were the ones that escorted the senorita and her beau to Freddie's spread."

Joshua returned a sour expression.

"What'd you want them to do … leave them at the entrance so she'd give birth in the dirt?"

Joshua replied without blinking, "They could've just as easily driven them to the hospital in Fort Stockton."

"And risk the senorita giving birth on the interstate?" Pepper's eyes blazed, "Joshua, what's gotten into you?"

Joshua relented with a shake of his head. He returned his gaze out the windshield.

Pepper put the truck back in gear and mumbled, "Besides, they said something about the border police being hot on their trail."

"The border patrol … Pepper?!"

"Now, now, calm down, Joshua. The Apaches at the gate told them they hadn't seen anyone."

"So, they lied to the border patrol!"

"It wouldn't be the first time. You done it yourself. Remember back when Freddie's grandparents came to visit?"

"That was how many years ago … before we struck oil, Pepper! And Freddie's grandma wasn't pregnant!"

"It's not that big a deal, Joshua. You know the fed's mandate nowadays … see no evil, hear no evil. Hell, if they turned themselves in after they crossed the Rio Grande the Feds would've probably ended up driving them here themselves."

"Then why didn't they?"

"I told you. She's nine months pregnant. She wanted to give birth with her family around her."

"Well then, why the hell are you taking me over there? I ain't gonna deliver her baby."

"Freddie wants to ask you if they can remain here—"

Joshua shook his head trying to cut him off, "No!"

"At least until they sort out the legal situation."

"No!"

"He's already reached out to an attorney."

"I said NO! We let them stay here after lying to the border patrol, and they find out they're here … then every time an illegal crosses the border within 50 miles, they'll be at our gate with warrants. You can just drop me off at the stables and go tell him I said no."

Both men noticed a pickup racing towards them from the direction of Lil Mexico.

Joshua tipped his hat back a bit more on his head, "What now?"

The pickup skidded to a halt in front of them causing Pepper to stop. Freddie Gonzalez jumped out of the driver's seat and ran over to them. Joshua noticed a very nervous young man still sitting in the passenger seat.

That has to be, what's his name … Rito?

Pepper rolled down his window, "What's goin' on?"

Freddie, a short stocky Tex-Mex wiped the sweat from his brow, "My grandniece is going into labor and my wife said she thinks the baby could be breech. She don't think we have time to call a doc. Then I remembered, isn't Katy on property checking that steer for TB with Benny?"

Joshua was caught by surprise, "Katy's where, doin' what?!"

Pepper took his phone out and tapped on a number, "She is." He held a finger up, "Snake, it's Pepper. We got an emergency at Freddie's place. We gotta find Katy and send her there quick. Isn't she with Benny? You know where they are? Good, go get her and race her over to Freddie's."

A voice came from Pepper's walkie-talkie. It was one of the guards at the main gate, "Pepper, we got a problem. Border Patrol is back. The officer in charge says he knows the two are here. He said he's waiting for some backup then he's comin' in whether we open the gates or not."

Pepper glanced over at Joshua who glared back at him, before grabbing a rifle from the back seat and jumping out of the cab. "You and me are gonna have a conversation, Pepper, but right now, something ain't right. Those agents shouldn't have come back, not so soon, anyway. I'll take Freddie's truck to the gate. You run Freddie back home."

Pepper stuck his head out the window, "Joshua, you're in an ornery mood this morning. Don't be shooting up the border patrol."

Freddie jumped in next to Pepper then yelled out the passenger window as an afterthought, "What about Rito?"

Joshua climbed into the driver's seat next to the frightened young man. He hollered back, "He comes with me!" then floored the gas pedal.

As the pickup raced down the dirt path, Joshua gazed at his passenger until he was satisfied the young Mexican wasn't going to do anything foolish like try to jump out.

The young man finally found enough courage to ask a question in very broken English, "Are ju going to turn me into Federalis, señor?"

Joshua looked over at him, "You speak English?"

Rito shook his head, "No good."

Joshua switched to Spanish, "Creo que los agentes federales están corruptos. Cuando llegamos a la puerta, quiero que permanezcas en el camión. ¿está entendido?" (I think the federal agents are corrupt. When we get to the gate, I want you to remain in the truck. Is that understood?)

"Sí señor."

Joshua returned his full attention out the windshield, "And son, if you intend on remaining here, learn English."

"Sí--," Rito corrected himself, "Yes, sir."

* * * * *

As Snake's grandson, Benny Vela patted the steer to calm it, Katy Jacobs pinched the animal's neck to check its skin density before sticking it twice, injecting the steer with tuberculin.

Katy handed the hypos to Benny as they both watched a pickup race up to them, "We'll check this one for lumps in seventy-two hours."

Benny put the hypos away in his bag, "I know Pepper wanted us to check this steer, but shouldn't we tell Joshua?"

Katy kept her eyes on the pickup, "If there's a problem with that cow, we'll tell Pepper and Pepper will tell Joshua. I'm not bringing that man any more bad news."

The truck ground to a halt. Katy stood her ground, "What brings you out here, Grandpa? Checking on your grandson?"

Snake jogged over to them. Benny hugged his grandfather. Snake smiled, before turning to Katy, "Freddie's grandniece has gone into labor and my wife already left for town early this morning with the rest of the women. You two are the closest we have to midwives. Come on, I'll drive you out there."

Katy didn't move, "Where's Joshua?"

Snake put his hands on his hips, "Joshua had to take care of a problem at the gate."

Katy mimicked him, putting her hands on her hips, "What kind of problem at the gate?"

Snake took her by her arm, "Katy, let's go. I'll explain it all on the way."

* * * * *

Snake pulled up at Freddie's ranch with Katy and Benny at the same time that Pepper pulled up with Freddie. Katy headed right for Pepper, "Snake told me Joshua had to take care of some problem at the gate with the Border Patrol ... something to do with Freddie's grandniece and her husband? I think you better take a ride out there."

"Joshua sent me here. If he wanted me with him at the gate, he would've told me so."

"Pepper, that man can't be trusted if he loses his temper. Remember what happened when that motorcycle gang trespassed?"

"Now, now Katy, that wasn't Joshua's doing ... that was the Apaches. Besides those motorcycle thugs had it comin' to them. They were armed and drugged up and threatening to rape all the Apache women. Not a smart thing to do in front of the Apache men."

Katy shot back a suspicious glance, "Those Apaches wouldn't lift a finger unless Joshua okayed it. No one on this ranch would."

A groan came from inside. It was Carmen.

Pepper thumbed over his shoulder, "Don't you think you better get in there?"

Katy let her eyes remain on Pepper for a moment longer before barking out orders to everyone around her, "All you men … stay outside. I'll call if I need you."

She started inside then stopped, "Benny, you come with me. Ever deliver a baby before?'

Benny hurried inside after her. The men all laughed when they heard him reply from inside, "Sure, but only babies with four legs."

CHAPTER 2

THE DOUBLE-J RANCH – MAIN GATE
PECOS COUNTY, TEXAS
MORNING

The heavy-set Border Patrol agent shook the sturdy iron gates at the main entrance to the Double-J ranch, "I'm an agent of the United States Border Patrol. Now, open these damn gates, Tonto, before I place you under arrest for obstruction!" The agent's name tag read, 'Herrera'.

An Apache named Joaquin swept his long braids back with his hand and grinned, "You must be new around here, Kee Mo Sah Bee. The United States ends at these gates. This is Joshua's Country, jefe."

Border Patrol Agent Ivan Herrera was, indeed, newly-transferred from Yuma, Arizona, where he left under suspicious circumstances. Up until a month before, he was under investigation for drug trafficking and conspiracy to possess controlled substances with intent to distribute. The investigation screeched to a halt when the lead investigator turned up dead in his car with two large caliber bullet wounds to his forehead.

Herrera wasn't a suspect in the murder, but the drug cartel for which he allegedly transported and sold narcotics, were. Still, his superiors at Yuma Station thought Herrera was guilty, so they transferred him. Per federal employment rules, it was all they could do. He would become someone else's problem.

Herrera turned to his deputy, "Agent Martin, what's he talking about? What the hell is Joshua's Country?"

Agent Angel Martin, a twenty-eight-year-old Border Patrol Agent, grew up not far from the Double-J. The area seemed to spawn young patriots.

Returning to his home after serving, like those from the Double-J, Martin had joined the Border Patrol after three tours in Afghanistan stationed at Camp Leatherneck with the 2nd Marine Expeditionary Brigade. Probably a combination of his local roots and his being a Marine, Agent Martin was one of the few employees of the government that Joshua Jacobs tolerated. Perhaps, he even liked the young man, though the old cowboy would never show it.

As for Agent Martin, he respected "Mr. J," as he called him. Before the arrival of Agent Herrera, Agent Martin's superior was another Agent who was born and raised in the area that Joshua tolerated, but he retired. Agent Martin thought he might be considered for promotion to the vacant position, but in the government's asinine opinion they thought he wasn't tenured enough.

Truth was Agent Martin wasn't very popular with Border Patrol brass. He was too patriotic and conservative for their politically-correct tastes. The fact he wasn't popular was almost certainly another reason Joshua respected the young man, not so much for his political views, but because he stood his ground.

So, in yet another brilliant move, the politically-correct government chose to place a possible criminal in the position, instead of someone that didn't toe the P-I line. Not being promoted didn't

bother Agent Martin half as much as having to work with and report to the arrogant ass, unconvicted criminal Agent Ivan Herrera.
He hated most being associated with the corrupt Agent because it
made him appear corrupt too, and that made him feel dirty.

Agent Martin nodded in the direction of the gate, "You're looking at it. Everything you see beyond that gate, as far as the eye can
see, in both directions belongs to Mr. Joshua Jacobs and his three
partners. The name of the ranch is the Double-J, but everyone in
these parts calls it Joshua's Country, 'cause beyond those gates, Mr. J
makes the law."

Herrera's look went from amazed to indignant, "What kind of
bullshit is that? Last time I checked a map, the U.S. border was
more than 20 miles from here, in that direction. That makes everything beyond that gate U.S. territory. Agent Martin, you're a federal
agent. You should know better than spreading bullshit like that."

"Bullshit or not, the people around here consider it a different
country on the other side of that gate. For as long as I can remember, Mr. J has been taking in folks that don't fit in on this side of the
gate … Apaches … Tex-Mexicans … black folk …. Skin color don't
mean a hill of beans to Mr. J and neither does formal education,
criminal records, religious convictions, or what team you root for
… that is, as long as it's the Cowboys.

"They say Mr. J only has two rules in his country … work hard,
and don't lie to him. All who abide by those two rules get paid well,
and get to live on his property as equals."

Herrera snickered, "So this country of his is filled with a bunch
of miscreants who'd probably rob him blind if they ever get the
chance …," Herrera nodded toward the Apache guards on the other
side of the gate, "like the Apache scum he's got guarding his gate."

Agent Martin's continence turned serious, "Those men would

die for Joshua Jacobs … and they'd kill for him too. Everyone in Joshua's Country would do the same."

Herrera stroked his chin, "That's right, didn't I read not long ago that a bunch of motorcyclists were last seen in the vicinity of this ranch? I bet if you went back to their teepees you'll find a motorcycle in each one. They probably took scalps too."

Herrera said his last few sentences just loud enough for Joaquin to hear. Agent Martin met the Apache's eyes while he replied to Herrera, "Those 'motorcyclists' were a rogue offshoot of the most notorious motorcycle gang in this part of Texas.

"Rumor has it that they showed up en masse at these gates just before midnight and tried to enter the ranch illegally. When the Apache guards confronted them and told them police had been dispatched, they laughed. Then they shot two of the guards and made a third open the gate at gunpoint. Before they tortured that third guard, they told him that they were gonna kill him and then head to the homes of all of the Apache to rape their wives and daughters and shoot their sons."

Herrera felt eyes on his back. He turned to find Joaquin staring darkly at him.

Agent Martin continued as Herrera and Joaquin's eyes remained locked, "The story goes that they threatened to chop that third Apache guard into little pieces while trying to keep him alive for as long as possible.

"They started with the pinky on his right hand, but that was as far as they got, because Mr. J showed up out of nowhere with the rest of the Apache in tow. The gang took off into the ranch, probably thinking they could motor to the other side and disappear into the night. Apparently, they didn't know just how large the ranch is. Well … they disappeared into the night, and that's the last anyone has ever heard or seen of them."

Herrera turned to Agent Martin momentarily showing faint fear in his face before wiping it off with his hand and turning back to face Joaquin, "Now, that's gotta be the biggest cock and bull—"

Joaquin was holding his right hand up for Herrera to count … one … two … three … four fingers – no pinky.

The color drained from Herrera's face as two more Border Patrol SUVs arrived on the scene. Four agents jumped out and hurried over. They greeted Agent Martin warmly, but only curtly nodded to Herrera.

Herrera grinned with the arrival of his backup, but the grin disappeared at the sight of a pickup truck racing towards the gate on the other side. He had a strong suspicion of who it was.

* * * * *

Joshua skidded to a halt thirty feet from the main gate, kicking up dust that momentarily enveloped the pickup. He took several seconds to survey the situation outside the gate before speaking in Spanish to Rito, telling him to climb into the backseat and keep down.

Joshua grabbed his rifle, exited the pickup, and motioned to Joaquin to open the gate. He approached Agents Martin and Herrera without uttering a word. Herrera spoke first, "And who might you be?"

Agent Martin offered his hand to Joshua, "Agent Herrera, this is Mr. Joshua Jacobs. Hello, Mr. J."

Joshua glanced at Herrera but spoke to Martin, "What brings you out here, Angel?"

"I brought him out here," Herrera answered the question. "We're looking for—"

"Angel, you know better than to just show up at my gate uninvited and without a warrant," Joshua cut him off.

Herrera stepped into Joshua's line of vision, "How do you know we don't have a warrant?"

"'Cause we wouldn't be having this conversation on this side of my gate if you did." Joshua's reply was curt as he stared Herrera down, before turning back to Martin, "Now Angel, you get rid of the rest of these badges and you and I can talk a bit."

"I'm in charge here!" Herrera pushed Martin behind him and stepped into Joshua's face. "My men stay and you'll speak to me … that clear?"

Amused, Joshua looked at Martin.

Martin answered the unasked question, "He outranks me, Mr. J. He's my boss."

Joshua turned back to Herrera. The chubby agent slipped his thumbs into his belt and pushed his belly out even further, "That means this is *my* country.

The agents behind Martin chuckled, which made Herrera smile, "Let me explain to you how this is gonna go. You're gonna order your Apache scum to step aside and let us pass, while you lead us to that pregnant puta and the mule she was traveling with. Then once we take them into custody, I may be generous enough not to arrest your ass too."

Joshua took a step back and let only his eyes turn to Martin. Martin wiped his mouth nervously.

Herrera's temper flared. He pulled out his badge and dangled it in Joshua's direction, "You see, I got the badge," he thumbed over his shoulder at the other agents who tightened their grips on their rifles, "and the firepower. So what's it gonna be, hombre?"

As quickly as he turned his eyes from Martin to Herrera, Joshua kicked Herrera's badge up and out of his hand, and while still in the air Joshua shot it with his rifle. The badge flew away about 30 feet.

Before his men could move and Herrera could draw his pistol, Joshua spun his modified Winchester model 1892 rifle and pressed the barrel under Herrera's chin, "Pull that gun and I'll blow your head off."

Herrera slowly raised his hands.

"Tell your men to drop their rifles and get back in their trucks."

Herrera nodded and the men complied.

"Now let me explain to you how this is gonna go. You're gonna stand still while I do the talking … that clear?"

Herrera nodded.

Joshua turned to Martin, "Angel, I don't think you know anything about why your boss is here, do you?"

"No sir, I don't rightly know."

"Then I suggest you and those men get back in your trucks and hightail it outta here."

Martin's eyes met Herrera's as he turned on his heels. The other men waited for Herrera to nod to them before they followed Martin's truck.

Joshua waited for the trucks to disappear then took the barrel from under Herrera's chin, "Angel doesn't know a thing about what you're really doing here, so he ain't a threat to you. If anything happens to that boy, I'll be comin' for you."

Herrera rubbed his throat and nodded.

"You said the boy was a mule, so I assume what you're really here for is the contraband you made him transport over the border. That would also explain why you don't have a warrant.

Herrera didn't reply.

Joshua turned and headed to the pickup. He thumbed over his shoulder to Joaquin, "Watch him."

Joaquin immediately raised his own Winchester and pointed it at Herrera.

When he reached the pickup, Joshua opened the back door and motioned to Rito to step out.

The young Mexican did so fearfully.

Joshua lifted Rito's shirt. There was nothing concealed underneath. He looked past Rito into the backseat and saw a small backpack. Joshua spoke in Spanish, "Es que su bolsa?" (Is that your bag?)

Rito nodded, "Sí señor."

Joshua pointed at the bag, "¿Alguien puso algo en su bolsa en México? Un paquete?" (Did someone put something into your bag in Mexico? A package?)

Rito's face lost color. He nodded, "Me habrían matado a mí y a Carmen si no hiciera lo que decían." (They would have killed me and Carmen if I didn't do what they said.)

Joshua took the bag and reached into it. He pulled one of six metal canisters out and opened it. It was filled with a white powder. He pointed back at Herrera, "Le dijeron que su entrega a ese hombre?" (You were told to deliver these to that man?)

Rito shot a quick glance in the direction of Herrera and terror filled his eyes, "Sí señor, pero él y sus hombres intentaron matarnos antes de que yo pudiera darle los botes. Carmen y yo corrí antes de que pudieran disparar contra nosotros." (Yes sir, but he and his men tried to kill us before I could give him those canisters. Carmen and I ran before they could shoot us.)

Joshua patted Rito's shoulder, "Regrese en el camión y espéreme." (Get back in the truck and wait for me.)

Joshua dumped the rest of Rito's belongings into the backseat leaving just the canisters inside the backpack and headed back to Herrera.

"The boy said you tried to kill him and his wife."

Herrera smiled, "Why would I do a thing like that?"

He handed him the bag.

Herrera studied Joshua for a moment before glancing inside the bag. He looked back up confused.

"You ever come back here, I'll kill you. You understand me?"

Wearing a smirk, Herrera tipped his hat and headed for his badge. As he leaned down to pick it up, the sound of a rifle report was followed by the badge flying off another twenty feet.

Herrera glared back at Joshua. Joshua responded by spinning his rifle once more and shooting the badge again, sending it out of sight.

Joshua spat on the ground, "You don't deserve to wear that badge."

Joshua headed back inside the gate. As soon as was in, Herrera rushed to pick up his gun. By the time he reached it, fifty Apaches were pointing rifles at him from inside the gate.

Herrera got into his vehicle and glared in Joshua's direction. As soon as his door closed, he raced away in a cloud of dust.

CHAPTER 3

THE DOUBLE-J RANCH – GONZALEZ RANCH
PECOS COUNTY, TEXAS
LATE MORNING

Joshua hadn't fully stopped the pickup in front of Freddie Gonzalez's home before Rito jumped out and ran into the house. Pepper, Snake, and Freddie walked over to the truck. Joshua rolled his window down.

Pepper spoke first, "Joaquin radioed Snake. He said the only thing you shot was some fool Border Agent's badge?"

Joshua ignored the question. He nodded towards the house, "How is she?"

"Katy won't let us in and she hasn't come out yet."

Joshua stepped out of the cab, "I want to talk to her."

"You still haven't heard from Josh?" Pepper knew Joshua's grandson had been in the habit of writing to his grandfather at regular intervals. Usually Joaquin would retrieve all the mail for the ranch and deliver it to Joshua, but not when Josh was deployed.

From the day young Josh would ship out until the day he returned home, every morning Joshua would ride his horse, *Trueno* to the mail box outside the gate and wait there until the mail truck came. This latest deployment was young Josh's fifth in as many years. At an average of eight months per deployment, that amounted to almost 1,200 days in harm's way.

Joshua knew, as all Marines do, there are only so many times you can dance with the devil and be able to walk away. Still, in his correspondence and conversations with Josh, he was not going to pressure his grandson. He wouldn't risk damaging his relationship with Josh as he did with his son, James. Instead, Joshua just prayed in silence at Sarah and James's graves and tried not to worry. "Let go and let God" was most difficult for a Marine as well as a cowboy.

When young Josh was deployed, Joshua breathed a sigh of relief with every letter he received, and every time his grandson returned home, instead of coming on strong, Joshua would lay back. He'd go fishing and hunting with him on the ranch. The result was just what Joshua wanted. Josh always talked about the ranch in his letters like it was the place he couldn't wait to return to.

Even better, in his last letter, just weeks ago, Josh finally intimated that he might be ready to leave the Corps when his current tour of duty was up. He mentioned that in his next letter he would let his grandfather know whether he would reenlist or not. Yet, it had been almost a month since Joshua had heard from Josh.

Joshua walked over to Snake, "Contact Joaquin and tell him to keep a keen eye out at the gate. And while you're at it, put some of your braves at the refinery on double duty. I want a few more security squads out there to roam the ranch."

Snake nodded, "You expecting that Border Agent to return with his men ... with or without a warrant?"

"I ain't expecting him to return at all."

"Expect the best, prepare for the worst," Pepper added. "Isn't that what I taught all of you?"

"That and the difference between our rifles and our guns," Snake winked as he grabbed his crotch.

Joshua grinned. Pepper remained straight-faced.

A pained grunt then a cry of joy came from inside the house, followed by the cries of a baby. Within moments, a teary-eyed Rito emerged from the door with his newborn son in his arms wrapped in an Apache blanket. He held the baby out for a moment and looked to Heaven before the men joined him. Joshua remained behind them and kept his distance.

Pepper pushed the blanket from the baby's face. Freddie asked for a blessing on him in Spanish before kissing the baby.

"What's his name?" asked Snake.

Rito walked over to Joshua and held the infant so that Joshua could see his face, "His name is … Joshua," he said in broken English. "We name him after you, señor." Rito handed the baby to Joshua.

Joshua looked down at the baby and his mind flashed back to when he held James the same way. All he could manage was a raspy, "Muchisimo gracias."

He noticed everyone looking at him with tears in their eyes. He quickly handed the baby back to Rito.

Katy stepped up from behind the men wiping her hands on a towel. She nodded towards the door at Rito, "It's time for Mama to feed her baby."

Rito kissed Katy's cheek before disappearing into the house. Katy walked over to Freddie, "It was a difficult delivery. Your grandniece should really go to the hospital—"

She cut herself off from Freddie's vigorous shaking of his head, "… but she can stay here, as long as she remains in bed. I'll come and check on her a little later."

"My wife and the other women should be here any minute.

They will look after Carmen." Freddie kissed Katy and hugged her, "Thank you, Katy."

Benny walked out of the house. He nodded to his granddad then called over to Katy, pointing to his bag, "If I'm not needed here anymore, I better get going."

"I'll see you back at my clinic. Thanks Benny," she replied.

"When will he get the results?" Joshua asked from behind her.

Katy's eyes met Peppers. He raised his eyebrow.

She turned around and folded her arms, "I was under the impression that you didn't know—"

"Katy, you should know better than that," Joshua cut her off, "there ain't nothin' I don't know about, on my ranch."

She slapped the towel over her shoulder, "Then why did Pepper contact me instead of you?"

Joshua looked over at Pepper who cringed from his reply, "Occasionally, I have to let the old man do something … helps him keep his wits sharp."

"Who you calling 'old man'? And as for my wits, at least I can remember where I put my cell phone."

"I remember where I put it. I keep it in my saddle bag."

Pepper tossed Joshua his cell phone, "You know you have to charge cell phones, right Joshua?"

Joshua caught the phone, looked at it a moment then tossed it back, "That's why I employ you, ain't it?"

Pepper's nostrils flared as he turned and started for his pickup, mumbling the whole way. When he reached the door he called out, "Katy, you need a ride somewhere?"

She was about to reply when Joshua grabbed her arm, "I'll give her a ride, Pepper. You just go charge my phone."

The phone sailed through the air. Joshua strained to catch it.

"Charge your own damn phone!" hollered Pepper as he kicked gravel up and sped away.

Katy shook her head and headed for Joshua's truck. They entered the cab and Joshua started the engine, but didn't put it into gear.

"Joshua, if you know why Pepper called me, you know it takes three days to receive TB test results back."

"Huh …? Oh yeah. I know. Katy, have you heard from Josh lately?"

She took the towel from her shoulder and put it between the seats. Joshua could tell she was trying to maintain a calm disposition, but she wasn't doing a very good job of it.

"I talked to him by phone a couple of weeks ago. He said he was looking forward to coming home soon."

"He told me the same thing in the last letter he wrote me. He also said he's thinking of not reenlisting."

Katy looked fiercely at him.

"Don't look at me like that. I didn't say a word to him."

"You don't have to say a word. He adores his grandpa."

"I love that boy, Katy. You know that. And I wouldn't risk what happened between me and James. But if he wants to leave the Marines and take his place here on the ranch, I'm sure as hell gonna welcome him."

"With what, the keys to that damn house?"

Her words kicked Joshua in his chest.

"I'm sorry, Joshua. I'm just not sure his dad would be happy with him moving into that house and taking over here."

"His dad is dead, Katy. My son is dead, and so is my wife. That leaves only you and Josh as my next-of-kin."

"Listen to me, Joshua Jacobs. James was my husband and Josh is *his* son and mine. If there are anyone's wishes he should honor, it's ours, not yours, no matter how much you try to bribe him with."

"First, I never bribed my grandson, nor would I ever, and second ... Josh is a man now. He'll make up his own mind what he wants to do."

"Right ... with you dangling the keys to that house and this *kingdom* in front of his eyes.

Joshua didn't feel anger. He felt frustrated and ... something he hadn't felt in a very long time. He felt hurt, the same hurt he felt long ago when James walked out on him.

"Katy, you and I haven't had words in so many years ... why are you saying all this?"

"Because it needs to be said now, Joshua. James used to idolize you, like Josh does now. But by the time James and I got married, you were an overbearing tyrant. The more this damn ranch grew, the more your ego grew.

"You crushed James's self-esteem and made both of us miserable. We hated being here because we hated being around you. Did you know that? You made us feel worthless ... like we couldn't get on without your handouts."

Joshua blinked with pain in his eyes, "I was proud of what I was building for all of us. I just wanted James to respect it."

"James didn't respect it. He was proud of the ranch, but he didn't respect it. He respected *you*!

But, did you respect him, or his wishes? No, you didn't! You scolded and berated him and threatened him ... as if being cut out of your will was being banished from God's kingdom!"

Joshua didn't reply.

"James loved this ranch, almost as much as he loved his father, but you drove him from it. And worse, he joined the Marines and stayed in because he wanted to emulate you ... no, he wanted to best you."

Tears sprung from Katy's eyes, "Well, he bested you alright. They returned him in pieces!"

Joshua's eyes reddened with tears. He reached out to comfort Katy. She welcomed it for a moment before pushing his hand away, jumping out of the cab and slamming the door.

Joshua jumped out and followed after her, "Katy ...! Wait ... where you goin'?"

"Anywhere, as long as it's away from you." She stopped and turned to face him, "I'm not going to let you destroy Josh like you destroyed James. If it weren't for Sarah, you wouldn't have even known your grandson. Did you know that? The only reason I let him see you was to honor her wishes."

"Katy ... I've changed since then. You've seen it with your own eyes, haven't you?"

She stared pitifully at him.

"I mean, you and I've learned to work together over the years, haven't we?"

She smirked with sarcasm, "Have we, Joshua? Have we really? Or is the way we 'work' together, by giving each other a wide berth? The truth is we can't stand each other."

"That ain't the truth! I love you ... and Josh." Joshua was as surprised as Katy was that he blurted that out.

Katy's smirk returned as she shook her head and walked away.

Joshua didn't follow her this time. He shouted after her, "You've never forgiven me, Katy! That's what this is all about! You blame me for James's death!"

"You're right, I do!" she yelled over her shoulder as she waved her arm dismissively and ran into Freddie's house.

Joshua was left standing there alone. A tear finally managed to find its way out of his eye and onto his leathery cheek. He blinked the rest away and whispered to himself "I don't forgive myself."

CHAPTER 4

AL ASAD AIRBASE - DFAC
HEET, IRAQ
NOON

Sitting alone at one of the mess tables, Sergeant Joshua Jacobs II put the finishing touches on a letter, sealed it, and handed it to a young Private First Class standing behind him.

"Thanks for mailing this, Russ."

"Not a problem Sarge."

Young Josh took a bite of a chicken tender as he addressed the next letter he was going to write, this one to his mother, when he heard someone calling him. It was Lance Corporal Reggie Arrington, an African-American native of West Philadelphia.

"Yo, Sarge … you gotta come out and see this!"

Josh took a sip from an apple juice container before replying, "See what, Reggie?"

"You ever see the movie, 'The Mummy'? The one with that mutha of a sandstorm, like a wall of sand …? Well, that shit is heading our way!"

Josh gave the tall Lance Corporal a doubting look as the loudspeaker came alive with two high-pitched beeps, "All personnel on base, if outside seek shelter. If inside, remain where you are, no one on the road, only emergency vehicles."

"I wouldn't jive you, Sarge. Now, come on … you have to see this shit!"

Joshua shoved a whole chicken tender in his mouth then stuffed the envelope he just addressed into his shirt pocket, before rising and following Arrington outside. He couldn't believe his eyes. Both men froze and looked north.

They saw a billowing brown wall rising a thousand feet into the air and stretching out for miles in each direction. Its approach appeared slow but relentless. Every place it reached disappeared into it, as if the blob was alive and hungry and all-consuming. As it neared, it grew ever taller, wider, darker, and more ominous.

As Josh stared at the storm, the hairs on his neck stood up. Something wasn't right. There was malevolence about it.

When he was a child, Josh remembered Uncle Snake telling him nighttime tales of the Apache monster, Big Owl, a man-eating ogre who would appear when storms came. After hearing those stories, he watched storms approach from the prairie with fear in his eyes. He hadn't felt that fear since he was a boy, until now.

Arrington was aiming his phone at the storm, which just reached the outer perimeter of the air base.

"Let's get inside, Reggie."

"Hell no, Sarge, I'm gonna capture this mama on camera!"

The storm seemed to suck up sound until it reached the base. Then the howling of wind started to pick up. The wind reached them before the sandstorm did. It was gale force and getting louder every second.

The air became hazy. Josh could see people running to various shelters. Some seemed to disappear in the middle of the road. Then

the sky began to get dark. The darkness crept over the base just as
the sand had, until everything became pitch dark. Josh held his
hand out in front of him and couldn't see his fingers.

Josh's fear turned to panic. He looked for Arrington but he
couldn't see anything.

He yelled out, "Reggie, we gotta get inside now!"

Josh heard Reggie's voice, "This shit is whack! Wait until I post
this shit on YouTube!"

Suddenly beams of light pierced the total darkness. Josh turned
to see hundreds of light beams aiming in all directions.

Aiming …?!

Josh hit the ground as he yelled out, "Reggie, hit the dirt!"

The crackle of gunfire burst out from all over the base. Josh
could hear bullets whizzing over his head. Still unable to see a foot
in front of him, he could do nothing but lie there. He heard screams
coming from all around him, followed by men yelling to each other
in Arabic.

Slowly, the gunfire died out as the darkness started to lift. In
the haze, Josh could see figures holding Kalashnikovs. He could
see now that the light beams were coming from simple flash lights
taped to the rifles. Quickly, he reached down and pulled the plastic
tip off of one of his shoe laces. Concealed inside was a thin tapered
metal shim, one and a half inches long, something Snake taught
him.

Thanks, Uncle Snake!

He placed the shim into his mouth and used his tongue to bend
it into the contour inside his bottom row of teeth.

As the haze followed the storm out of the base, Josh could see
bodies lying about throughout. He turned to see Reggie lying face-
up with a bullet hole in his temple. His camera was lying next to his

body.

Before he could turn again, Josh felt a hard steel barrel being jabbed into the back of his head. He remained on his knees and put his hands up. Two men, wearing all black with their faces covered by balaclavas stepped in front of him. The taller of the two spoke in Arabic to the other one who then lifted Josh to his feet.

The taller one switched to British-laced English, "You are now a prisoner. Obey and you will live. Resist and you will die."

Vehicles of all sorts began pulling up. Josh saw a number of other base personnel, at least a dozen or more men and women, both Marines and Air Force, all with their hands on their heads, being herded into the vehicles. Joshua felt a gun barrel poke the back of his head. The tall one waved towards the lead vehicle with his rifle, "Move."

Josh was pushed into the back. The tall one got in the front passenger seat, lowered the window and waved his arm. The convoy raced forward on his command.

CHAPTER 5

Joshua stood next to Trueno patting him on the side of the road. Joaquin came out from the guard shack and walked over to him, "Mr. J., I could bring you the mail the moment it comes. You don't have to come out here each morning."

Joshua kept his eyes down the road, "Then who'd be watching the gate while you're bringing me the mail?"

"I could call for a runner."

Joshua spotted the mail truck in the distance, "Trueno needs to stretch his legs every morning, anyway."

Joaquin nodded and turned to see a pickup racing up from inside the gate. Pepper kicked up dust skidding to a stop in front of the guard shack. He jumped out, leaving the ignition on and the driver door open while heading straight for Joshua. Joshua kept his eyes peeled on the mail truck that was now only one-hundred yards away.

"Joshua …!"

Joshua never took his eyes off the mail truck, "Pepper, there's only two places I don't want you to bother me ... three if you count the bathroom—"

"Joshua ... its young Josh!" Pepper held out his cell phone.

Joshua spun around quickly. He stared at Pepper a moment before taking the cell phone from his hand. The screen showed a FoxNews.com headline that read, "ISIS ATTACKS AL ASAD AIRBASE," under the headline it read, "Hundreds massacred and a dozen taken hostage from ISIS 'Storm Demons' attack from within super-dust storm!"

Joshua looked up from the screen in shock, "Josh...?"

Pepper took the phone from him, used his finger to page down and handed it back to him. Joshua saw photos of the hostages. His heart stopped when he saw a photo of Josh in his dress blues.

Pepper took the phone back, put his arm around Joshua and turned him towards the truck, "We should go to Katy. I can't get her on the phone."

Joshua tried to blink away the shock. He nodded as they both rushed into the pickup with Pepper behind the wheel. Joaquin called out, "I'll take care of Trueno, Mr. J!"

The pickup raced right past the mail truck which just arrived. Joaquin approached the mailman who pointed back at them, "What's their rush?"

Joaquin ignored the question. He just took the mail, and called for a runner to bring it to Joshua's house.

CHAPTER 6

PECOS COUNTY ANIMAL HOSPITAL
PECOS COUNTY, TEXAS
LATE MORNING

Katy Jacobs exited the surgery dressed in bloodied blue scrubs. She was surprised to see Joshua and Pepper standing in triage. Then it occurred to her. She walked past them removing her blood-soaked surgical gloves and tossing them in a biowaste trash receptacle, "The test results aren't in yet, and you being here won't speed them up."

Pepper approached her, "Katy, we've been trying to call you."

"I've been in surgery all morning. An eighteen-year old quarter horse found his way onto the interstate. He was fortunate to only be hit by the side-view mirror of a pickup—"

"Katy," Pepper cut her off, "we need to talk to you, in your office."

Pepper's tone sent a chill down her spine. She looked over at Joshua and saw he was upset. There was no color in his face.

The last time I saw him looking like that was at James's funeral.

"Josh …! Something happened to Josh?!"

The sound of a news broadcast coming from the waiting area drew her attention. She ran to it. Pepper and Joshua ran after her.

The people sitting in the waiting area were startled by her bursting through the doors still wearing her bloodstained scrubs. She ignored them, running to the TV monitor mounted to one of the walls. She fumbled for the remote and turned up the volume.

"... *Fighters attacking an Iraqi base. More than three-hundred Marines were stationed there. Reports coming in are now saying that over one-hundred personnel of the Al Asad Air Base, in Heet, Iraq have been killed in what has been coined, 'The Sandstorm Massacre,' carried out by the notorious 'Storm Demons,' one of the most violent and successful units of ISIS. It is also believed the infamous leader of the Storm Demons, Shakir al-Wahi who has been video-taped committing dozens of beheadings, personally carried out the attack ....*"

Pepper caught up to her first, "Katy ...!" He tried to turn her away from the TV monitor, but she pulled out of his grasp.

The screen changed to the same set of photos that Joshua saw on Pepper's phone. Katy's eyebrows rose in horror.

"*Along with the dead, the White House has just confirmed that at least twelve base personnel were taken captive, a combination of Air Force, civilian personnel, and Marines.*"

Katy grabbed her forehead and stumbled backwards. Joshua caught her. He spun her around and hugged her tightly. She buried her face into his shoulder and wept.

"They'll behead my son ... Joshua! They'll behead Josh!"

Joshua pulled her head from his chest, "Shhh ... Katy, we won't let that happen."

Katy's continence changed from sorrow to anger, "*We* won't let that happen? Isn't that what you said about James?!"

Katy's words were like daggers to Joshua's heart. He took his hands from her. His pained look fueled Katy's rage even more.

"Get out ... get out of here and don't come back!"

Joshua stepped back and lowered his eyes before turning to leave. Katy shouted after him, "Did you hear me … don't come back!"

She whipped around only to find Pepper standing there staring down at her, a combination of anger and sorrow in his eyes. No words were exchanged as he walked past her and followed Joshua out the door.

CHAPTER 7

THE DOUBLE-J RANCH – JOSHUA JACOBS HACIENDA
PECOS COUNTY, TEXAS
EVENING

Joshua sat on a chair in the living room staring at the glass of amber spirits in his hand. A bottle of Jameson eighteen-year-old Limited Reserve Irish Whiskey sat atop the end table next to him. The TV was muted and turned to a blonde Fox News anchor discussing where the hostages might have been taken, with two military analysts.

Pepper stood near the window reading the captions, "The notorious Shakir al-Wahi, leader of the mythical, terrifying Storm Demons … the media make them sound superhuman. No wonder so many think they're unstoppable."

Joshua sat quietly.

Pepper went on, "They're the enemy, nothing more, nothing less. The sooner everyone realizes that, the sooner those animals can be wiped out."

Pepper saw that Joshua was in no mood for the discussion, so he returned to peering out the window. He saw the headlights of a pickup.

"Someone's coming."

Joshua didn't even look up from his drink.

Pepper shrugged from frustration then walked out of the room, went to the front door and opened it. Snake and Freddie entered. Freddie spoke first, "We just came from Katy. I left my wife, Carmen, and Rito with her."

"I thought Carmen wasn't supposed to leave the bed?" said Pepper.

"Yeah, well, I figured if something goes wrong, who better to be with than Katy. Besides, she brought the baby with her. I was hoping little Joshua might lift her spirits some."

"How's Katy?" The question came from Joshua, now standing at the entrance to the living room. The three walked over to him. Freddie hugged him before replying, "She calmed down a bit before falling asleep. Only took one bottle of tequila. She was already exhausted."

Joshua nodded.

Freddie wiped his chin nervously, "Joshua … some of the people at the hospital told me and Snake how she snapped at you. You know she didn't mean none of that. She was just … well you know how she feels about young Josh."

Joshua flashed a quick glance at Pepper before replying, "I know." He walked over to Snake, "Do me a favor, send Joaquin and another brave over to her house. Have them make their presence known then remain outside and tail her wherever she goes."

"Will do," replied Snake as he glanced at his cell phone.

"Tell them to keep the reporters and any other strangers away from her … got that?"

"Got it," replied Snake before talking into his phone.

"I sent Benny over too. I told him to try and take over any of her duties that he can handle at the animal hospital."

"Good thinking," replied Joshua. "Thanks amigo."

Snake ended his call and walked over to Joshua, "Joaquin said he had your mail delivered this morning and Trueno was stabled. He said he had the mail put ...," Freddie walked over to the staircase and picked up a pile of mail, "right here." He handed it to Joshua.

Joshua thought about putting it down, but rifled through it, as a matter of habit. His heart went into his throat when he came across a handwritten envelope with the top line of the return address reading, "2nd Marine Expeditionary Force." Joshua knew the handwriting.

Pepper noticed the look on Joshua's face and walked over, "What is it?"

"It's a letter ... from Josh." The three men gathered around him.

"Well," said Pepper, "aren't you gonna read it?"

Joshua took a seat on the stairs and opened the letter then reached into his pocket and put on his reading glasses.

Dear Gramps,

I am writing this letter while sitting in the mess about to eat chicken tenders to be washed down with apple juice. Boy, do I miss those steak and beer dinners on the ranch!

You know my current tour is about up and so is my enlistment. Well, I wanted you to be the first to know that I have decided not to reenlist."

A flood of emotions overcame Joshua. Pepper sat down, put his arm around him and took the letter from his hands. He put his reading glasses on and read the letter aloud. Joshua listened carefully when Pepper caught up to where he left off.

"I haven't told my mother yet. I'm not sure how she will feel about it. I mean, I'm sure she will be happy I won't be placing myself in harm's way anymore, but I'm not sure how she will take what I'm going to say next.

Grandpa, I would like to come work for you and take that place you always talked about my having on the ranch. I hope it is still available to me.

I can't wait to see Mom and you, and Uncle Pepper, Uncle Snake, Uncle Freddie, and everyone else. I miss home. I always considered the Double-J my home.

Get your hunting rifle and fishing rod ready. Not much going on here, so I hope to be home in a few weeks.

Love,

Josh

p.s. Don't tell Mom. I will write her as soon as I finish eating.

Pepper put his glasses away and wiped a tear from his eye. He noticed Snake and Freddie wiping their eyes too.

Pepper folded the letter, put it back into the envelope, and handed it back to Joshua, "I wonder if he ever wrote that letter to Katy."

Joshua stared straight ahead for a long moment before replying in a raspy whisper, "I don't know." Then he stood up, walked up the stairs, and disappeared into his bedroom.

"Pepper, what you think about young Josh's chances?" asked Freddie.

Pepper put his finger to his lips and glared back. He motioned for Snake and Freddie to follow him into the living room where he poured two fingers each of whiskey into three glasses and handed one to each. Pepper didn't drink, so they didn't drink.

"I don't rightly know young Josh's chances, Freddie. From what I read, it seems that those towel-headed bastards ransom some and murder some, with no real rhyme or reason put to it. They butcher their own kind as much as they do us. Women … children … old … young … none of it matters to them."

Snake and Freddie looked demoralized. Pepper noticed and added, "But there are a couple things we do know. We know Josh wasn't killed on base, and if we can believe the news reports, we know he's been taken hostage. Now there ain't but two reasons for them to take hostages … to trade them for ransoms … or to make public spectacles of their murders."

Pepper invoked his old drill sergeant tone, "So, until I tell you boys otherwise, we will believe the former. Is that clear?"

Both answered in unison, "Aye aye, Sir!"

Pepper waited for his cheek to stop twitching before raising his glass. Snake and Freddie raised theirs.

"Semper Fi!" barked Pepper before downing his.

"Semper Fi!" they echoed and downed theirs.

The men looked up at the TV monitor as photos of previous ISIS hostages were being displayed. Snake quickly grabbed the remote and paused the playback on a photo of one of the handcuffed hostages. The three men drew nearer to the screen to examine the image more closely.

After a moment, Snake pointed to the handcuffs, "If they put them on young Josh he may have a chance."

Pepper raised a brow, "I seem to remember his Uncle Snake teaching him all sorts of escape tricks when he was a kid."

"Damn right," replied Snake with a grin. "You never know when the pale face are gonna slap cuffs on you."

His grin disappeared, "I hope those lessons stayed with him."

CHAPTER 8

CONVERTED SCHOOLROOM
OUTSKIRTS OF DEIR AL-ZOUR, SYRIA
NIGHT

Young Josh opened his eyes and saw the same blackness as when they were closed. He blinked several times to make sure they were open then turned his head to see the smallest sliver of light bleeding from under what must be the door. He was lying on a dirty bare floor wearing only the filthy jihadi clothing, a partially buttoned shirt and pants with an elastic waistband.

He got to his knees and tried to stand but immediately fell wincing in pain.

I remember now ... they hung me upside down and whipped the bottoms of my feet to prevent me from trying to escape.

Falling to the floor also reminded him that two particularly sadistic guards beat him with a pipe and tortured him with a cattle prod. Jolts of pain from the back of his head and his back started flooding into his brain.

He heard footsteps and voices speaking in Arabic growing louder outside the door. A key was being inserted and then the door was flung open.

A flood of bright light blinded Josh as he felt himself being lifted to his feet. He was flanked by the same two guards wearing those familiar black balaclavas concealing their faces that had tortured and beat him. He knew they were the same from their eyes. A grimy sack was placed over his head and his wrists were handcuffed behind his back.

Tears escaped his eyes from the jolting pain from his mangled feet as he was dragged from the room. As his sight came back, Josh noticed the room had a small blackboard on the wall at one end.

Looks like this was a classroom ... was this a school?

The guards dragged Josh up a flight of stairs and down a corridor. He was pushed to the left and felt his shoulder bang into what felt like a doorframe to another room ...

The Dean's Office ...

He joked to himself. The guards forced him down into a chair and removed the sack from his head.

Josh realized he was sitting in a solitary chair facing a dilapidated wooden desk. Seated at the other end of the desk was a fierce-looking man with powerful features. Josh realized at once what was different about him from all the others.

This one doesn't conceal his face.

Josh surmised that the man was easily as tall as he was, around six feet two inches, but the man was burly, perhaps twenty pounds heavier than him. Long, flowing jet-black hair descended from a light brown turban on his head and connected to an equally long, flowing jet-black beard. The man was wearing all black, draped clothing with a light brown utility harness buckled over from his shoulders to his waist. A Kalashnikov assault rifle sat upon the desk.

There were two masked guards standing to the left and right of the desk, while the two guards that brought him into the room stood behind his chair to the left and right. The man casually examined objects lying on the desk in front of him. Josh realized at once that they were his belongings – his wallet, dog tags, uniform, boots, and utility belt.

The man began examining the contents of his wallet. He dumped the money in it on the desk, examined both sides of his driver's license before dropping it onto the money, and then smiled when he saw the photo Josh kept behind his driver's license.

The man took the photo out and after examining it closely for a few moments, turned it to face Josh. It was a photo of him standing between his mom and grandfather at his high school graduation.

"These are your parents … yes?"

Josh didn't reply.

Without warning he felt the butt of a rifle impact the side of his head. The blow almost knocked him out of the chair. The other guard quickly sat him up. Joshua winced away the pain.

"My name is Shakir, you have heard of me, yes?"

Josh shrugged his shoulders, "Nope."

Shakir looked genuinely upset, "And your name is …," he picked up Josh's driver's license, "Joshua Jacobs. So, you are Jew and American."

Josh paused before replying. He looked up at the guard who had rifle-butted him, "I'm a Texan."

The guard looked for permission to smash Josh's head again, but Shakir shook his negatively.

Shakir leaned forward resting his elbows on the desk and curled his upper lip into a brutish grin, "Texas, yes, John Wayne and the land of cowboys."

Shakir lifted another item from the desk, this time an envelope. Josh knew what it was.

The envelope I was going to use for the letter to my mom ... damn!

"You resemble the woman in the photo too much, Cowboy. Her name is ...," Shakir read the envelope, "Katy Jacobs, care of Pecos County Animal Hospital."

Shakir dropped the envelope onto the desk, rose to his feet and came around to stand in front of Josh, "You are impressed with my English, yes? I learned it while imprisoned by U.S. forces in Tikrit.

"I spent six years in an American-run jail in Saddam Hussein's hometown before being liberated. While there, a Christian missionary taught a few of us English. When I was freed by my brothers, that missionary was the first Christian I beheaded."

The guards standing behind Josh laughed. The other two remained quiet. Shakir pointed to the two that laughed, "They were imprisoned with me. They also were taught English by the missionary. They held him down while I beheaded him."

Josh displayed none of the revulsion he felt.

Shakir leaned down so that he could speak softly into Josh's ear, "You were going to send your mother a letter, yes? I will send one for you. First, I will ask for a ransom for you. How much should I ask for? Is your mother wealthy?"

Josh could tell the two behind him were about to bash him again with the butts of their rifles, so he replied, "My mother is an animal doctor."

One of the guards behind him said something in Arabic which made all of the men in the room laugh.

"Abdul said that all American doctors are animal doctors, because all Americans are pigs."

The guards behind him laughed again.

Shakir grabbed the envelope from the desk, "I shall ask for the cash equivalent of a quarter kilogram of gold, the sum I am entitled to by the laws of Islam.

But whether it is paid or not, I will behead you and send the video to your mother with a message telling her that we now know exactly where she lives, and works, and that we will be paying a call on her sometime soon."

Every muscle in Josh's body tightened. This time he couldn't withhold a display of his anger. Shakir comprehended the fiery look in his eyes and sneered.

Shakir barked orders in Arabic as he exited the room and instantly the two guards behind him hurried after him, while the two guards behind Josh lifted him from the chair and dragged him outside. Josh concentrated on keeping his wits about him.

He left his rifle on the desk.

Josh noticed the first two guards were now standing behind a video camera set up on a tripod. The camera was pointed in the direction of a small wall that was covered by a giant green screen. The two guards dragging him forced Josh to his knees about ten feet in front of the camera. They held him there while Josh watched Shakir approach pulling a ten-inch black-handled, serrated blade from a scabbard hanging from his harness.

Shakir placed his open hand on Josh's head and dismissed the guards holding him down.

Shakir looked down at Josh, "First, we make a video for the world to see ... an American cowboy defeated by the Indians, yes ... John Wayne on his knees. Then we will make another for your mother.

He barked an order to the guard operating the camera and waited until the guard nodded before bending Josh's head back and placing the knife to his throat.

Shakir spoke in Arabic. Several times he pulled the knife away in order to point it at the camera, before returning it to Josh's throat. The one thing Shakir didn't say in Arabic was the only thing Josh could understand, the name John Wayne. For a moment, Josh recalled watching John Wayne movies with his grandfather. Despite the situation, the memory made him smile softly.

I'm being compared to the Duke. Gramps would be proud.

Shakir ended his tirade with the familiar call, "Allahu Akbar!" His men echoed his words in a unified shout before the guard working the camera again nodded. Josh watched as the guard pulled what looked like a memory stick from the camera and handed it to Shakir. Shakir smiled at Josh as he held the memory stick up and shook it before handing it to another of his guards who ran off with it.

Shakir sauntered over to Josh with his arms crossed, "That guard will take the recording to one of our technicians who will add a background to it. It will be released on the internet within the hour. There will be no way to trace it back to this location, but even if they did, we will be moving as soon as we make the second recording."

Josh spit sand from his mouth, "Do you always share this much information with your captives?"

Shakir furrowed his brows but quickly followed with a grin, "No, I do not, but you intrigue me, Cowboy. I have long waited for a prisoner like you. Most that we capture are so filled with fear, by the time I begin slitting their throats they are more like birds than people.

"Some believe it is good for the world to see the fear on the faces of our defeated enemy as I behead them. But, I think it would be more effective to show the world the face of a defiant one ... like you Cowboy, so that the world can see how defiance turns into cowardice as my blade slowly severs your head."

Shakir leaned down to speak directly into Josh's ear, "The coward cowboy will make me even more famous."

A black-clad fighter emerged from the building yelling in Arabic and pointing to the sky. Everyone looked up in all directions, but no one saw anything. Suddenly, a rumbling sound like thunder was heard by all. Shakir began waving his arms and shouting to his men.

Before anyone could move, Josh saw a streak of light soar out of the sky and hit the roof of the building he thought was a schoolhouse, followed instantly by an incredibly loud explosion that emanated from deep inside the building. The force of the blast knocked everyone to the ground. Fireballs blew out of the windows incinerating a few of the men standing closest to the building, followed by chunks of brick and debris raining down on everyone else.

Still on his knees and uninjured from the explosion, Josh found himself the only one not lying face down on the ground, including Shakir, who had been pelted with large shards of building material.

That missile could've come from the Syrians, the Iranians, or the Americans. Whoever it was ... thanks!

As quickly as he could, Josh spat out the metal shim then fell backwards towards it. Clawing with his hands, Josh sifted through the hard desert sand trying to find it, while never taking his eyes off Shakir. Slowly, the large man rose to his knees with his back to Josh.

Where the hell is it?!

Josh saw Shakir turning back towards him. He closed his eyes and held his breath, trying to appear unconscious.

Shakir got to his feet with knife in hand and walked over to Josh. Josh heard his footsteps then felt Shakir kick him hard in the side. He did his best not to flinch.

Josh heard voices in Arabic and the sounds of men running in his direction. He chanced opening his eyes just a sliver in time to see two of Shakir's men pointing at the remnants of the building, now billowing thick, black smoke. Shakir began shouting orders at them.

It's now or never!

Josh started raking the sandy ground with his fingers until something sharp pricked his thumb. He strained to pinch the thin metal sliver just as Shakir and his two men turned to look down at him. Shakir barked more orders and his men reached down and lifted Josh by his arms. Josh feigned being seriously injured, allowing his legs to collapse and forcing Shakir's men to drag him hurriedly in the direction of a Toyota Hilux.

As nimbly as his Uncle Snake taught him, with his right hand, Josh inserted the shim into the cuff around his left wrist, raising the ratchet. The cuff opened with just a slight tug.

While one of the men opened the rear door, the other tossed Josh into the back of the pickup truck. After folding his legs inside, they slammed the door closed. Josh wasted no time, reaching over his head, opening the passenger-side door and falling out. Peering underneath the pickup truck, Josh saw legs belonging to Shakir joining the legs of two of his men.

Time to bug outta here, but where to??

The thick acrid smoke that poured out of the destroyed remnants of the building started floating all around the SUV. As casually as he could, and holding his breath, Josh rose to his cut-up bare feet and walked directly into the plume.

The silhouette of Shakir passed right by him heading for the passenger side front seat. It only took a moment before Josh heard Shakir hollering at the top of his lungs.

Aware he could only hold his breath a little longer, Josh hurried into the thickest area of smoke. Reaching the shattered ruins of the building, he began to feel heat.

Where there's smoke there's fire!

Unable to see anyone behind him, he heard the voices of Shakir and his men getting closer. There was only one direction to go – into the building. Covering his face, Josh finally took a breath, with his nose buried into the fold of his elbow before jumping over the rubble of the outer wall and entering.

The heat became more intense. After a few steps into ever-thickening smoke, Josh saw the source of the fire and smoke. There was an inferno rising from the basement.

That's where they were keeping me. I would have been toast!

Josh began hacking and coughing from choking on the smoke. He heard voices shouting in Arabic in every direction and thought he heard the sounds of groaning.

I think there are survivors in this hell hole.

Josh headed away from the flames and eventually found himself in what looked like the corridor outside the room where he first met Shakir. The smoke and heat were less intense, but it was still difficult to know for sure. The roof had mostly collapsed into the structure, taking with it most of the inside walls and doors. Rubble and debris covered everything.

Josh could hardly stand on his badly-lacerated feet.

If I can just find my boots!

The sound of movement from behind prodded him forward. Pushing splintered planks out of the way, Josh entered what he thought was the room he was in with Shakir. He froze when he heard the deep moaning sound of ceiling joists beginning to buckle overhead.

I can either die standing still or looking for my boots. I choose the latter.

Josh slogged through the thick rubble. Through breaks in the smoke he could now see black-clad men behind him, inside the cindered ruins, as well as others running about outside. He continued to push through the mire until he noticed something familiar.

That's the chair I was sitting in!

Josh did his best to pick up the pace, though every step caused intense pain, until he reached the chair. He sighed in despair when he looked ahead.

All my things, along with Blackbeard's rifle were sitting atop the desk!

In front of the chair, where the desk used to be, the entire area of ceiling and wall had caved in. Josh began pulling chunks out of the large pile. Suddenly, he heard footsteps behind him. He hit the floor, pulling a large panel of what he thought was the front of the desk on top of him and froze.

Two fighters waded into the room sweeping their assault rifles in front of them. All Josh could see was their black boots getting closer and closer. They stopped only inches from him.

Josh heard them speaking to each other then he began hearing pounding sounds – the sounds of rifle butts being smacked into the pile of debris just over his head. Josh covered his face with his hands and waited for the inevitable. After the sixth blow it happened. The pile gave way like an avalanche.

The good news was it chased the two fighters out of the room. The bad news was that the bulk of the debris fell onto the panel he was using to conceal himself.

Josh waited until he didn't hear any sounds nearby then tried to move. Every time he tried, he heard the avalanche start again, and when he heard it, he stopped moving until it stopped.

Finally, he decided to try one large push-and-roll. For a few terrifying moments, Josh thought the sky was falling, as a seemingly endless amount of objects, large and small, pelted his wooden panel shield. He choked from all the dust and dirt that followed until he realized the barrage had ended.

With one last push, Josh dislodged himself and was able to get to his knees. He grinned when he saw the outcome. The large pile that had been sitting on the desk was now dispersed all around it, and the first familiar objects he saw were his boots.

Josh reached for them then realized that he was still holding the shim in one hand and had the cuffs dangling from his right wrist. He used the shim again to free himself completely then quickly snatched his boots before returning the shim into his mouth. To his delight, he found his socks stuffed inside the boots. Putting both on, he stood up and found the pain to his feet was barely tolerable.

Josh began searching the mess around him until he found Shakir's rifle. He shook it to clear the barrel then checked the curved magazine.

Fully loaded, thank you God! Now, how do I get outta Dodge?

Josh headed back into what was the corridor. Once again, he heard voices coming from the direction of the blaze and groans coming from further down the corridor. He headed towards the sound of the groans and found a black-clad fighter pinned under a piece of the collapsed roof.

Blood soaked through the balaclava, Josh was still able to see the man's eyes. He was conscious and terrified.

He knows I'm a prisoner.

Carefully, Josh lifted a portion of the collapsed ceiling that was crushing the man and slipped the man's rifle under to brace it. Then, with care, he pulled the man out from underneath. The fighter grimaced in pain. Josh knew the man had to be suffering from multiple injuries.

As gently as he could, he began undressing the man. When the man started to cry out, Josh grabbed his rifle and pointed it at him. Josh put his finger to his lips, "Shhh."

The man complied. It seemed like it took forever, but Josh was finally able to don the man's clothes, including his blood-soaked balaclava. Josh could taste the man's blood. It sickened him.

The man's eyes began closing. Josh quickly slung his rifle and lifted the man over his shoulder. He carried him fireman-style out the back of the destroyed building. The moment he emerged outside, a dozen fighters hurried over.

I hope my blue eyes don't give me away!

Josh handed over the now unconscious man while the rest of the fighters spoke to him in Arabic. Josh wiped the blood from the balaclava onto his hand and showed them then coughed.

Hopefully, they think I was wounded in the throat.

One of the men pointed towards a caravan of vehicles, a mixture of SUVs, straight trucks, and cars. Josh nodded and started off in that direction.

There has to be at least two hundred men packing into those crates!

Josh reached the line of vehicles. It stretched out in front of him in both directions. He looked toward the front of the convoy and saw the other hostages from Al Asad Air Base being loaded into the back of a truck. They all had hoods pulled over their heads and they were handcuffed.

What would John Wayne do ... aww hell!

Josh made his way near the back of the truck. The chaos of the situation was an advantage to him. Most of Shakir's men were piling into the vehicles, while a few others stood guard around the caravan. Josh positioned himself like one of the guards which gave him an ideal vantage point.

He counted eleven hostages sitting in two rows inside the truck. They were joined by fighters armed with AK-47s sitting against the back wall. An additional two fighters stood guard just outside the back.

Three white-but-muddy Toyota Hilux pickups in front of the truck were packed with fighters and they looked like they were about to leave, but the head SUV had its front passenger door opened.

They're waiting for someone … Shakir?

He had another thought.

Those damn trucks are made in Texas.

He took a deep breath.

If I'm gonna do something, it has to be now!

Josh slipped next to the side of the truck, said a silent prayer then shot the rear tire with one round from his rifle. The tire exploded and hissed until it was flat.

Instantly, the guards from the back of the truck appeared. They were joined a few seconds later by the driver and another fighter from the cab.

Josh pointed frantically to a ridgeline at the end of a barren patch of desert. Before anyone could ask questions he wouldn't have understood, Josh dropped to one knee, took aim, and started firing at the ridgeline. Without hesitation, the men around him did the same. A one-way firefight ensued.

In less than a minute, a familiar voice was shouting in Arabic. The men ceased firing. Josh turned to see a group of fighters bounding over. In their midst was the one hollering … Shakir.

He approached one of the fighters who had been guarding the back of the truck, and as far as Josh could tell, was asking him what the hell the shooting was about. The fighter pointed in Josh's direction and for a moment, his heart stopped, until he realized he was pointing beyond him.

Josh stepped out of the way and the man pointed again, this time directly at the shot-out tire. Then, he pointed out to the ridgeline.

Shakir walked over to the tire and inspected it then looked out to the ridgeline with an incredulous gaze. He approached the fighter who explained the situation to him and barked some orders. The fighter pointed at his counterpart who had been guarding the back of the truck and both took off running into the field.

He's sending them to inspect the ridgeline.

Next, Shakir spoke to the driver and the other fighter from the truck's cab. Josh watched as they hurried to get the truck's jack and lug wrench.

He ordered them to change the tire. Uh-oh, I'm the only one left!

Shakir stepped in front of Josh and spoke in Arabic. Josh squinted to try and conceal his eyes. Shakir noticed the blood on his balaclava. He said something in Arabic to which Josh just nodded weakly.

I hope I got that right!

Shakir grabbed Josh by the arm and led him to the back of the truck.

What now ... did I blow it?!

Shakir called the two fighters out of the back of the truck. They jumped down and came to attention. Shakir turned to Josh and spoke in Arabic. When Josh didn't move, he nodded into the truck and pushed Josh towards it.

I think he wants me to get in. Here goes nothing ....

Josh climbed into the truck and took a seat where the two guards had been sitting, against the back of the trailer. Shakir continued to stare at Josh until he pointed his rifle at the prisoners. Finally, Shakir nodded and walked off.

Josh peaked out at the guards.

They're more interested in the ridgeline than what's going on back here.

He spoke in a loud whisper, "Listen to me and don't speak."

His words caught everyone's attention. He could tell they were all facing him now.

"I'm a Marine from Al Asad. I was taken prisoner with you, but I've escaped. I'm trying to come up with a plan to free y'all, but it ain't gonna be easy. We're sitting in a truck in a long train of enemy vehicles and I can't speak Arabic, so I can only guess at what's happening. The building we were being held in was bombed ... I have no idea by who—"

"The Syrians ...," the man closest to Josh was the one who spoke. Josh quickly glanced out the back of the truck. The guards were nowhere in sight. He yanked the hood off the man.

He looks Middle Eastern.

"I'm Airman First Class Gabriel Nahas, Sir. I'm an Air Force Linguist stationed at Al Asad."

Josh took the shim from his mouth and undid the Airman's cuffs, "I'm Sergeant Josh Jacobs, Airman. How do you know it was the Syrians?"

"Sir, I heard the ones that escorted us to this truck talking. They said a Syrian fighter jet fired the missile, but they also said that the Americans were spotted less than ten klicks from here, on the ground, heading in this direction."

"That must be why we're bugging out so quickly," Josh thought out loud.

A shout in Arabic was heard outside the truck. Airman Nahas pulled the hood over his head, "The fighters outside are being ordered into the truck. They're pulling out."

As he spoke, the two fighters standing guard outside the back of the truck climbed in. Josh returned the hood to Nahas's head then pulled a knife from the utility belt he was wearing and concealed it by his leg, as the fighters made their way to him.

One of them said something to him in Arabic. Josh shot a look at Airman Nahas which confused the fighters. For an instant no one moved, until the truck was heard being put in gear.

As the truck leapt forward, Josh sprung up from his seat and thrust the knife up and into the throat of the closest fighter to him. Taken completely by surprise, the fighter collapsed to the floor with the knife still wedged deeply under his chin.

Confused, the second fighter didn't react right away. Josh reached over and took him in a headlock. Frenzied, the fighter clawed at Josh's arm. Unable to dislodge it, the fighter pulled his own knife and stabbed Josh in his forearm. Biting his lip so he wouldn't cry out, Josh could no longer hold the fighter in the headlock.

The fighter's head butted Josh, sending him falling back onto the bench behind him. The fighter raised the knife over Josh, but before he could slam it down, he froze. The fighter's eyes opened wide from pain, before he collapsed on top of his comrade. Josh saw why. His knife was protruding from the fighter's back.

Nahas was standing behind the bodies, "Good thing you undid my cuffs. Are you alright, Sarge?"

"I'll live. Hand me your hood."

Nahas picked up the hood he'd been wearing and handed it to

him. Josh cut a two-inch strip from the bottom of it and wrapped the strip around the wound to his forearm.

Nahas tied it tightly, "What now? We're moving."

Josh looked behind him and put his hand against the heavy tarp being used to enclose the back of the truck. He pulled his knife from the back of the fighter and after wiping it clean on the dead man's back, he cut a foot-long slit in the tarp. Peeking through the slit, Josh stuck his head out then pulled it back in.

"There's a back window to the cab. Two fighters are sitting up there, the driver and an AK-wielding passenger."

Josh pulled the shim from his mouth and began freeing the others, letting them pull their own hoods off, "For now, keep the hoods on your laps, just in case."

"You got a plan, Sarge?" asked Nahas.

Josh stood a moment staring at the slit he cut in the tarp. Nahas and the others looked at it, perplexed. Finally, Josh pointed at the dead fighters, "Nahas, switch clothes with the one you iced."

Josh turned to the largest of the others, "What's your name?"

"Lance Corporal Klimkowski."

Josh raised a brow, "Marine …? I don't know you. Who you with?"

"SP-Mag-Taff."

"So am I, Lance Corporal."

"I was just transferred from Morón two days ago."

Josh nodded, "Bad timing. Welcome to Iraq, Lance Corporal. Do your best to squeeze into the other Ali Baba's blacks and dress him up with yours."

"Aye, Sarge."

Nahas put the balaclava on, "What's the plan, Sarge?

"The cavalry is behind us. We gotta try and make it to them."

CHAPTER 9

Border Patrol Agent Ivan Herrera entered the crowded saloon and took a seat at a table. He slung the bag with the drugs in it behind his chair then casually stretched. A cute blonde waitress wearing an apron tied around a tight dress and cowboy boots, walked over, "What can I get you?"

"Two Negra Modelos."

"Two …," the waitress winked, "you expecting company or just real thirsty?"

Standing behind her, a swarthy Mexican wearing a black leather jacket over a red buttoned shirt and bolo tie slipped his hands around the waitress's waist and kissed her neck.

The waitress didn't need to turn around, "Leo … I told you not to do that when I'm working!"

Leocadio Lozano, one of the Zeta cartel's captains, flashed a dimpled smile and took a seat across from Herrera, "I will be joining this gentleman for some drinks."

He slipped a hundred dollar bill into the waitress's belt, "Also bring the bottle of Gran Patrón Platinum I had you hold special for me and two shot glasses."

The waitress's eyes sparkled. Lozano smacked her rear, "Go on!"

Herrera looked around. The place was noisy and festive, "I tell you I don't want to be seen with you, and you pick this place?"

Lozano sat back in his chair then snapped his fingers, "Give me the bag."

Herrera couldn't help looking around before grabbing the bag and placing it on the chair between him and Lozano.

Lozano returned a sarcastic smirk before taking the bag into his lap and opening it. He looked inside nonchalantly then closed it and placed it back on the chair.

It amused him to see the nervous look on Herrera's face, "Relax amigo. We meet here because no one around us cares what we're doing. They are too busy unwinding from their boring lives and trying to get laid."

Herrera stared at the bag, "You're just gonna leave it there? I don't like it." He looked around again then leaned in and spoke softly but sternly, "You better not think you're gonna pay me out in the open!"

The waitress returned. She put the beers down first followed by a black velvet bag. Herrera could hardly keep his nerves in check as she untied the bag and slipped it down, revealing the elegant, clear bottle of tequila.

Lozano slipped his arm around her waist, "I will do the honors, Señorita." He spanked her bottom again, "Leave us. When you finish your shift, come by the hotel."

She winked at him and walked away.

Lozano picked up the bottle and threw the black bag to Herrera, "I will pour. The bag is yours."

Herrera looked curiously at Lozano then into the bag. He took a key from it.

"The key is to the locker at your gym. Your reward is inside a tote bag."

"My locker …?"

"Si, amigo," Lozano handed a filled shot glass to him then clanked his against it, "Salute." Lozano downed his shot. Herrera did the same.

Lozano poured another two shots, "You should know that we know everything about the people with whom we do business, including where they exercise. And it just so happens that I work out there too, sometimes."

Herrera downed his second shot then took a sip of his beer and started to stand.

"Where you going, amigo, we still have business to discuss."

"What business?"

Lozano downed his second shot. This time he only poured another one for himself, "Any problems with this last shipment?"

"Problems … not really."

Lozano sipped his shot, "Not really … from what I heard, you almost lost the whole shipment."

Herrera leaned in trying to keep his voice down, "Who told you that?!"

"I told you … we know everything." Lozano chuckled, "That gringo on that big ranch made you look like el Tonto. I heard you even lost your badge."

Herrera's face turned red, "I should've killed him."

Lozano poured Herrera another shot. Herrera drank it and slammed the glass down.

"Easy, amigo … with the money you can make, soon you can

buy a solid gold badge."

"Can make ...," Herrera looked sideways at him, "you got another job for me?"

"Si ... another job, but this time there are no bags for you to lose. Fifty amigos would like to visit the Alamo. Trouble is they can't cross the border without your help."

Herrera let a smirk grow on his face, "That all ..., fifty, you say?"

"Si."

"So you want me to finagle fifty wetbacks—"

"I don't like that phrase, amigo. After all, I am one of them. With a name like Herrera, I would think you would find it offensive too."

"I was born in Chicago. I don't speak the language and I don't like the food."

"Your loss, amigo." Lozano pointed to the expensive bottle of tequila, "At least you like the liquor. In any case, I never said they were Mexican and with the money you will be paid, it shouldn't matter to you whether they're from Mars."

"How much?"

"Five thousand a head. They'll come across in groups of ten, staggered over the next three days. "

Herrera shook his head, "Five groups of ten in the next three days ... what's the rush?"

"That's none of your business."

"Where are they gonna go? That many will be spotted if they move in groups."

"Again, none of your business ... but I can tell you ... arrangements have already been made for all of them. Now, amigo, every one of them will be traveling with backpacks. Those backpacks cannot be inspected by anyone, including you."

"This ain't my first rodeo. Besides, I could care less which drugs they're running. They are running drugs, aren't they?"

Lozano stared at him.

Herrera scratched his chin, "None of my business … right. So, you want me to facilitate fifty non-Mexican illegals crossing the border with backpacks, over the next three days with no questions asked. That's gonna cost you more than five thousand a head."

"How much more?"

Herrera thought about it, "More like twenty-five thousand a head."

Lozano finished his drink then put the cap on the bottle and pushed it across the table, "Seven thousand a head and you can have the rest of the bottle."

Herrera was quiet.

Lozano leaned in, "Amigo, don't overestimate your value … or your safety."

Herrera put his hands around the bottle, "Seven thousand per is fine, half before, half after."

Herrera leaned closer, "One more thing, amigo … each time I do a job for you, I send a sealed envelope to an out-of-state law firm with directions to place the envelope into a safe deposit box under my name. Inside each envelope are the details on each job you send me, along with your name as the person who sent me on the job, and your ties to a certain Mexican cartel.

"Each month, I also take a selfie of me sitting at my desk, at the homeland security office in El Paso, which I then email to the same law office. They have instructions that if they don't receive the email with my selfie, they are to take all the envelopes from the safe deposit box, for which they have a key, and make copies of their contents. Then they are to send the copies to various news media outlets, as well as to the local and federal authorities."

Lozano remained silent and didn't blink.

"Now, you might say, that's not real evidence against you, amigo, but I'm sure you'd agree that your cartel friends will not be so happy with you if all those details are made known tying them to you, and you to me. So, for your sake, I better never go missing."

Lozano sipped his beer, tossed five more hundred dollar bills onto the table and stood, "That's for our bill. Half the money will be in your locker, along with a throw-away phone. A call will be placed tomorrow at 7 PM ... your instructions, dates, times, and locations. Make sure you don't miss that call. The other half will be paid the same way when the job is done."

Herrera waited until Lozano had walked out the door before opening the bottle and pouring himself another shot.

CHAPTER 10

THE DOUBLE-J RANCH – JOSHUA JACOBS HACIENDA
PECOS COUNTY, TEXAS
EVENING

Joshua sat alone on the rear balcony watching a news report on a small TV. The reporter was wearing a flak jacket and helmet and was reporting from somewhere near the Iraq-Syrian border. The screen suddenly changed to a video clip of a man on his knees. A fierce-looking man with long black hair and beard was holding a knife to the kneeling man's throat and speaking in Arabic as a translation was typing out on the screen. Joshua's heart sank when he saw the face of the man on his knees.

Pepper walked out onto the balcony with a bottle of whiskey and two glasses. He put them on the table then stood behind Joshua's chair. He placed his hand on his friend's shoulder and watched with him.

As soon as the report concluded, Joshua muted the TV, "The bastard called him John Wayne. He didn't refer to any of the others that way. Why Josh?"

"Maybe he got it from Josh's accent," replied Pepper as he filled both glasses and placed one in front of Joshua.

"So, you think the bastard knows the difference between a New York accent and a Texas accent?"

"What you drivin' at, Joshua? What difference does it make?"

Joshua thought about it, "The difference is that terrorist bastard made it personal between him and my grandson … and that could cost Josh his head."

Pepper downed his glass and tried to change the subject, "I checked in with Freddie. He said Katy sent his wife and Carmen home, but he and Snake are keeping tabs on her, and Benny is helping her at the animal hospital. Snake cut her cable so she can't watch TV. Then the cable man showed up and Snake explained to him that nothing was wrong with it. He got the message."

Joshua took a sip of his whiskey and nodded. He got up, walked to the railing, and gazed up at the moon. Pepper joined him, "If they wanted to kill Josh, they could've done that already. The ones they videotape … don't they always ask for a ransom?"

Joshua blinked his reply, "They do, but they've also been known to murder their prisoners whether they ask for a ransom or not."

Pepper looked confused, "Then what's the purpose-?"

"The purpose is," Joshua cut him off, "to terrorize the families and friends of the victims, along with the rest of the God-fearing world … and to humiliate and demoralize anyone they consider an enemy."

Joshua dropped his gaze from up at the moon to down at his boots, "The atrocities they're committing have been committed before."

"You mean what the Nazis did in World War Two?"

Joshua nodded, "But long before the Nazis, the Romans fed Christians to the lions in the Coliseum. Buying a ticket and watching the savagery was considered a pastime … like going to watch a sporting event. Nowadays, the terrorists videotape their atrocities and upload them to the internet. Some people watch and are sickened … others watch and are fascinated. But, not enough are motivated to action."

Pepper nodded, "It don't hit home for most here. It's happening to people they don't know in a faraway land."

Joshua walked back to the table. He picked up his glass and took another sip as both men watched a newsfeed of a long convoy of vehicles filled with black-clad terrorists waving their weapons in the air.

Joshua finished his glass and set it down, "Ironic … those pickups they're driving are made here in Texas.

"Something tells me it won't be long until they strike here … people they know in their own towns."

Joshua turned the TV off and patted Pepper on his shoulder before walking inside.

Pepper watched him leave then said out loud, "After what they're doing to his grandson … God help 'em if they come here."

CHAPTER 11

HIGHWAY
OUTSKIRTS OF DEIR AL-ZOUR, SYRIA
NIGHT

Joshua made another vertical slit in the tarp next to his first cut. The slits lined up directly behind the driver and passenger in the cab with only a rear window separating the cab from the tarped rear.

Joshua spoke to everyone in the rear of the truck, "We have to try and take control of this vehicle. Airman Nahas and I will take out the driver and passenger hopefully with one round each, fired simultaneously through the slits. As soon as we fire, we need to break away the remaining glass to the rear window of the cab."

Josh turned to Nahas, "Airman, once we fire and clear the glass, it'll be imperative that we pull their bodies through the window then take their places as quickly as we can. Lance Corporal, you then do your best to conceal the bodies and take a position seated on the bench. In case anyone looks back here, they'll see you guarding the prisoners. Clear?"

"Clear, Sarge."

"Sarge, as soon as we shoot them, what happens to the truck? We have to be traveling around forty or fifty miles-per-hour."

"I have no clue, so as quickly as I can, I'll try and get the driver's body out of the seat and my hands on the wheel."

"But if the truck stops? Almost all of the convoy is behind us."

"We'll just have to move as fast as we can, Airman. Failure isn't an option, no more than sitting here doing nothing. One thing's for sure … we won't have a fighting chance once we reach their destination."

Nahas took a moment before nodding. Josh turned to everyone else, "If we're successful, I'll be behind the wheel waiting for the best opportunity to make a break for it, but I can't be sure how I'll do that until I'm driving. Our forces are several miles behind us. If I can get this truck turned around, we might have a chance."

Josh paused, "The real trouble is that their leader is in one of the three pickups ahead of us. Y'all got a dose of him?"

Everyone nodded.

"So, it'd be best if we can break away without Blackbeard spotting us."

Josh paused again to look at each individual in the back of the truck, "Y'all on board with this?"

The replies were a mixture of, "Yes, Sir," and "Aye, Sir."

Josh nodded to them then nodded to Nahas. Simultaneously, both men stuck the barrels of their rifles through their respective slits – Josh aimed at the back of the driver's head and Nahas at the back of the passenger's.

Josh took aim, "You ready, Airman?"

Nahas's reply took a moment, "Ready Sarge."

"On three then … one … two … three!"

The reports from their shots sounded like one loud bang.

Josh turned his rifle around and began smacking the back window with it. It took a moment for Nahas to gather his wits and do the same.

The truck swerved a bit and worse, instead of slowing down, the truck was accelerating.

When the glass of the rear window was gone, Josh put his rifle down and reached into the cab. Instantly, the major problem with his plan became apparent. It was much more difficult than he thought to grab hold and move two dead bodies.

For the most part, they were traveling straight, but the truck felt like the dead driver was flooring the gas pedal. Rapidly, they gained on the pickup truck directly in front of them. The pickup was slow to respond. When it did, there wasn't much for their driver to do except get on the bumper of the pickup in front of them. One by one, the three pickups in front of the truck ended up bumper-to-bumper.

Josh and Nahas finally pulled the bodies from the driver's seat, but it was too late. The truck slammed into the pickup in front of it, which caused a chain reaction. The third pickup slammed into the back of the second, sending the second slamming into the lead pickup. The pickups all lost control and skidded in a zigzag pattern. Several fighters in the backs of the pickups were ejected. Their bodies bounced on the pavement. Meanwhile, Josh and Airman Nahas finally crawled into the cab and Josh brought the truck to a halt. They watched the chaos out the windshield.

Lance Corporal Klimkowski handed their rifles through the slits. Josh put his on his lap, "That didn't go to plan."

Airman Nahas held his AK in his hand, "You can say that again, Sarge. What now?"

They saw Shakir step from one of the crashed pickups. He was the easiest to identify, not only because of his long dark locks and beard but because he was the only one that didn't conceal his face.

Nahas tightened the grip on his rifle, "Speak of the devil, here comes Blackbeard. Sarge …?"

Josh turned, "Listen up, prisoners … hoods on, arms behind you. Lance Corporal … time for you to do your best silent-movie star impression."

"Aye, Sir," replied Klimkowski.

Josh turned to Nahas, "You do the talking if they ask questions. Just tell them the gas pedal got stuck."

"What if they don't buy it, Sarge?"

"Then you shoot and I'll drive. Clear?"

"Clear."

Shakir stormed over to the driver's side door trailed by six fighters. Josh slumped down and pretended to fiddle with the accelerator pedal.

Shakir spoke tersely in Arabic. Airman Nahas replied, telling him what Josh told him to say.

Shakir looked inside the cab with curiosity. Nahas saw what he was looking at – the blood stains and brain matter splattered all over the dash board.

Shakir opened the driver's door and uttered in Arabic. Josh looked at Nahas who mouthed, "Get out."

Josh stepped down from the cab and followed Shakir and his men to the back of the truck. The fighters pulled the tarp open as Shakir looked in. His eyes swept down the line of prisoners on both sides and fell on the large black-clad fighter seated on the bench against the inside wall. Something looked peculiar about him.

Shakir noticed the bottoms of the fighter's legs were exposed, as if he was wearing clothes that were too small for him. Then he noticed the fighter was barefoot.

Shakir started to raise his rifle when he felt a knife pressing against the side of his neck. His fighters didn't notice right away.

Josh spun the large man around and spoke into his ear, "Order your men back to their vehicles. Do it now or I'll press the blade right through your throat."

Shakir barked something in Arabic. The half-dozen fighters responded by pointing their rifles at Josh. The seventh was holding an RBG-6 six-round, revolver-type Grenade Launcher. He held the compact weapon pointed at the ground.

Josh pushed the tip of the blade into Shakir's neck. Blood flowed from the wound. Shakir barked again in Arabic. This time the fighters lowered their rifles, but now Josh noticed fighters from the pickup behind the truck starting to approach.

Josh hollered, "Nahas get your ass back here!"

The Airman left the cab and hurried to the back of the truck. He couldn't conceal the shock he felt from the scene.

Josh slipped his knife back into its scabbard and raised his rifle, pointing it at Shakir's crotch.

"Order those men back into their vehicle … now! And keep in mind, we understand your language."

Shakir raised his hands carefully and waved them at the approaching fighters as he shouted orders. The men stopped in their tracks and returned to the pickup.

"Now, tell these men to toss their weapons into the back of the truck."

Shakir kept his hands raised as he smiled and spoke in English, "Your eyes … is that you, Cowboy? It is, isn't it, yes?"

Josh didn't reply.

Shakir lowered his hands then put one to his wounded neck and dabbed at the blood, "Cowboy, what do you think you can accomplish? You are surrounded by a battalion of my men. All I have to do is cry out and you and all of your people will be cut down."

"If you do, you won't be able to have any fun with your seventy-two virgins, 'cause I'm gonna blow your dick off."

Shakir's smile disappeared.

"Now, tell these men to toss their weapons into the back of the truck, all but that one." Josh pointed to the one with the grenade launcher. He took the RBG-6 from the man.

Shakir hesitated then shrugged and issued the orders. The fighters moved slowly but obeyed, tossing their rifles, pistols, and handguns into the truck. Josh didn't have to order those inside to retrieve the weapons.

Josh waited for the weapons to disappear from the trailer floor, "Now, order them into the back of the truck, one at a time."

Shakir did as he was told and soon all the fighters had disappeared into the back of the truck.

Shakir's walkie-talkie came alive. "Sarge, they're asking Blackbeard what's going on up here," Nahas translated.

Josh took Shakir's radio from his belt and put it to his mouth, "Tell them … tell them another missile attack may be imminent and to standby until told otherwise."

Shakir looked strangely at Josh.

"Tell them!" Josh depressed the 'talk' button.

Shakir spoke. Josh looked at Nahas for confirmation. Nahas nodded. When Shakir finished, Josh let the 'talk' button up and placed the radio on his own belt.

Shakir looked defiantly at Josh as he held his neck wound, "What now, Cowboy? Do we stand here all night?"

"That's exactly what we're gonna do, my friend, but first you're gonna wave for the entire convoy to pass us and continue on to your original destination."

Shakir grinned sarcastically, "And you think my men will just leave me standing here with you?"

"Probably not … unless, of course, the convoy was under attack."

Shakir's expression changed to confusion, "Under attack?"

Josh raised the small grenade launcher, aimed it directly at the pickup behind them and pulled the trigger – once, then again, as the weapon was semi-automatic. The pickup burst into flames with two loud bangs. Fighters from the vehicles behind began shouting into the night.

Josh put the grenade launcher to Shakir's back, "Start directing traffic!"

Shakir understood, stepping around the blazing vehicle and waving to the vehicles behind to pass. Josh put the walkie-talkie back to Shakir's mouth, "Tell everyone that the convoy is under attack and to head directly to wherever you where heading."

Shakir's nostrils flared. Josh could see that the large man was reaching the end of his patience, but he still complied.

The bastard's arrogance was the only reason he was complying. He didn't think we had a rat's ass chance of getting out of this predicament. But, now he's not so sure.

The line—over a mile long—drove past the truck, as Josh and Nahas watched Shakir continue to wave his hands.

Josh turned to Nahas, "As soon as the last vehicle disappears down the road, turn the truck around. Then floor it and pray. I'll get in back with Blackbeard. I have a feeling he ain't gonna surrender willingly. As soon as he--"

As the last vehicle approached, Shakir jumped in front of it. It came to a screeching halt. Shakir started hollering in Arabic to the confused fighters in the pickup.

Josh shoved Nahas, "Turn the truck around and hightail it NOW!"

Nahas ran to the cab. Josh raised the grenade launcher as Shakir, still standing in front of the pickup continued to shout in Arabic. Josh took aim and pulled the trigger. Shakir noticed a split-second before and dove to the ground. The vehicle burst into flames with a loud bang.

About one hundred feet ahead, the vehicles at the end of the convoy skidded to a halt and fighters began pouring out. Josh heard Nahas yelling in Arabic to them. Josh saw them look up and duck back into their vehicles.

He must've told them we're under attack again. Way to go, Nahas!

Josh approached Shakir, "Get up!"

The large man didn't move. He was covered in shards from the exploded pickup. Small patches of fire burned just feet away.

Josh swung the grenade launcher around his back and aimed his AK at Shakir as he stood over him. He kicked the fallen man hard enough to partially turn his body. Josh saw what looked like a long, thin piece of the pickup's grill protruding from Shakir's side. The man's face was blackened with grease, pavement and ash. His eyes were closed and his face looked contorted.

Nahas turned the truck around. He pulled up parallel with Josh, on the opposite side of Shakir's body.

"He had it. Come on, Sarge, hop in! I told them it was another missile attack, but no telling if they'll decide to double back!"

Josh looked down the road. The last few vehicles were still there. A few were turned almost all the way facing them. Their headlights were illuminating the back of the truck. He gazed back down at Shakir.

I should put a round in his ugly head, but I can't chance it with his men looking this way. Time to bug out.

Josh lifted his leg to step over Shakir. In a burst of motion, the large man pulled the sliver from his side and stabbed it as hard as he could into Josh's thigh.

Josh collapsed in pain. With agility uncommon for a man of his size and in his wounded condition, Shakir grabbed at the grenade launcher and without aiming, pulled the trigger. A blast emanated from the muzzle with a flash and thud, and shot almost straight up in the air.

"Nahas ... GET OUT OF HERE!!" Josh yelled through gritted teeth.

The shell landed less than ten feet from the back of the truck. It exploded with a loud bang and a spark of light. Instantly, the pick-ups down the road started turning and heading in their direction.

Nahas put the truck in gear and floored the accelerator. The truck leapt into motion, as Josh tore the grenade launcher from Shakir's grasp. Simultaneously, Shakir pulled the knife from Josh's belt and plunged it into Josh's shoulder. Josh lost hold of the grenade launcher. He now had two weapons slung around him and two objects protruding from him.

Shakir pulled the knife from Josh's shoulder before Josh could get to it. With monstrous force, Shakir swung the knife down at Josh's chest, but Josh used every ounce of strength he had left to hold the man's arm up.

Shakir was gradually winning the battle of strength. In desperation, Josh let go of Shakir's arm with his left hand and used it to pull the long shard from his thigh.

As the tip of the blade began piercing Josh's chest, Shakir felt something long and sharp stab into his lower back.

Both men struggled to drive their weapons deeper into the other before finally succumbing to their wounds. Shakir collapsed onto Josh. For a moment, their mouths were next to each other's ears, as they each heard the sound of pickups skidding to a halt.

Shakir uttered a throaty whisper, "You have lost, Cowboy. Your mother will see me behead you, after all."

The faint sound of heavy rotors thundering in the direction of the Americans became audible. Shakir struggled to turn his head before turning back to Josh.

Josh was able to force a grin through the pain, "Big guy … you know what a Hellfire missile … outfitted with a thermobaric warhead … will do to you? The kill mechanism is unique … and unpleasant. The pressure wave … is gonna kill ya … but more importantly … before that, the subsequent rarefaction …"

Josh coughed up blood. His breathing was labored but he continued, "What I mean to say is … you're gonna be severely burned … all that long hair of yours … but y'all are also gonna inhale the burning gas."

Shakir stared at Josh. For the first time, Josh saw real fear in the fierce man's eyes as Shakir scanned the night sky.

"That's right … you're gonna cook from the inside out."

Black-clad fighters surrounded the two. They lifted Shakir up as the guttural roar of numerous AH-64 Apache helicopters grew louder in the night sky with their spotlights dotting the countryside and getting closer.

Shakir growled orders in Arabic which made a few of the other fighters reach down to lift Josh. They didn't realize that Josh had gotten his AK into his hands. Josh began firing and dropped one of the men.

Other fighters began running toward him, but the sound of the American choppers scared them back. Josh rolled over to face the direction of their retreat. He heard Shakir's voice bellow from the darkness, "I will have your head, Cowboy! And I know where your mother lives!"

The rifle fell from Josh's hands and his sight went blurry as the last of the pickups disappeared down the road.

CHAPTER 12

LAS BURRAS CANYON
TWO MILES WEST – BIG BEND RANCH STATE PARK
US-MEXICAN BORDER
DUSK

Agent Herrera sat alone inside his SUV. He pulled off the barren stretch of Farm to Market Road 170, just a quarter mile from the point where the last ten illegals were to cross into the U.S.

FM170 was the road closest to the US/Mexican border. It ran, more-or-less parallel with it. Though he was warned not to be nearby in the instructions he was given, Herrera's curiosity got the better of him. The knowledge he gleaned from his curiosity had paid off for him many times before, so he decided to pick a spot where he could watch the last crossing.

It was scheduled to happen at dusk. No specific time was given. His orders were just to keep all border patrol agents away from the area until the following morning.

Herrera decided to get to his concealed position an hour before. The crossings all took place at an abandoned "building with a red roof," as it was described in his instructions. Herrera reasoned that description was enough because there wasn't another building with a red roof for fifty miles in any direction.

He knew the location was chosen for its proximity to the Rio Grande which twisted in its path just a couple of hundred yards south of the building. Herrera also realized that the location was within two miles of the Big Bend Ranch State Park. He was curious about that.

Big Bend was one of the least visited state parks in the United States because of its remote locale. There were no border fences or checkpoints nearby, likely because anyone who crossed there would have to travel four hours to get to the nearest city. Though illegals wouldn't cross there, Herrera learned that drug cartels would, from time to time, which further made him believe that this was some sort of drug transport – a major one, by his reckoning. Still, the whole business seemed odd. He just had to see for himself.

Using binoculars, Herrera scanned the area near the building with the red roof and saw nothing. Not a soul. He checked the road again. Within the hour, in the distance, he saw a car approaching from the west. The car was nondescript in every way – five or six years old by Herrera's estimation, a compact Ford, not too clean, not too dirty.

Herrera focused on the driver as the car approached. It was a male, mid-twenties, dark hair, wearing a baseball cap. Herrera watched as the car slowed down and pulled off the road near the gate to the building with the red roof.

Herrera chuckled to himself, confidant that no one was there to pick up, "That's what you get for saying 'dusk' instead of an exact—"

Herrera cut himself off when he saw a man cross from the opposite side of the road and enter the passenger seat. The man was carrying a large backpack and a long leather case.

The moment the passenger door closed the car returned to the road, heading east. It passed him and, within a minute, disappeared around a bend.

Where the hell did he come from? I've been sitting here for an hour. I haven't seen so much as a lizard. That bag looked like a rifle case and that backpack … it almost looked … military-issued. Just one got in the car, what about the other nine?

Herrera returned the binoculars to his eyes and scanned the road. In the distance he saw another car approach. Again, it was nondescript, this time with an older man driving. The man wore a straw cowboy hat, but there was something familiar about his features, something that reminded him of the kid wearing the baseball cap. They had darker hair and features and could've been Mexican, but somehow, they didn't look quite Mexican.

This car did the same thing. It stopped in front of the gate just long enough for another person with an identical backpack and case to appear from a different spot on the opposite side of the road. That person also quickly entered the passenger seat, and like the first car, it too took off past Herrera in the same direction and disappeared.

Herrera watched as eight more vehicles, a combination of cars and pickups did, exactly, the same thing. All the drivers, save one, were male. Yet, even the sole female driver had very similar features to all the rest. Herrera thought they could've been central or South American, yet he couldn't be sure. He also didn't rule out the possibility that they could have been Middle Eastern.

Herrera knew it was too conspicuous to try to tail them on such a desolate stretch of road, so he waited there for five more minutes before taking off.

The passenger in the last vehicle noticed Herrera's SUV as they passed. He took a handheld device from his backpack, opened two apps – a translation program and the other to a game.

He signed into the game as "Roy Rogers," and looked in the game's lobby for another player named "Batgirl," then typed into the translation program. He typed in Arabic then copied and pasted the English translation into a direct message to Batgirl.

Roy_Rogers: Someone parked in SUV near red roof building. Watched us with binoculars.

Almost thirty seconds went by before the reply came.

Batgirl: Others took photos. They have been sent.

CHAPTER 13

PECOS COUNTY MEMORIAL HOSPITAL
FORT STOCKTON, TEXAS
MORNING

A doctor wearing scrubs entered the small waiting area located next to the surgery. Snake, Benny, Freddie, and Pepper were standing and behind them sat Joshua and Katy. Katy spotted the doctor and rushed over, with Joshua following.

"I'm Dr. Emerick. You're Josh's mother?"

Katy nodded nervously. She hadn't slept for twenty-four hours since receiving notification that Josh was being transported home. All she was told was that Josh needed immediate surgery upon arrival. They had all been waiting ever since, over six hours.

"I'm Katy Jacobs. How is he?"

The doctor noticed that Katy was also wearing scrubs, "Are you a doctor?"

"I'm a vet."

"I see. Well, your son arrived in critical condition. He had lost a great deal of blood and was in hypovolemic shock. He had severe puncture wounds that damaged his femoral artery in his thigh, as well as his lung.

I repaired the artery and the damage inside his chest cavity, but then his lung collapsed. After reinflating it, we administered a blood transfusion then norepinephrine to increase blood pressure."

Katy looked faint. Joshua reached out to support her, "Can we see him?"

The doctor nodded, "He's resting right now. He's been through a lot, considering the long trip here, followed by the surgery. We're going to want to keep him here for at least a couple of days to monitor for complications, especially due to the amount of blood loss Josh experienced.

"You look tired. Why don't you go home and get some rest. Your son will be asleep for several hours, at least."

Katy shook her head, "I'd like to wait in his room."

The doctor pointed behind him, "Through those doors, second room to the left."

Katy nodded.

Joshua extended his hand, "Doc, I'm Josh's grandfather."

Dr. Emerick shook his hand, "I know who you are, Mr. Jacobs."

"Would you mind waiting a moment?"

"Not at all."

Joshua waved Pepper over, "Take Katy to Josh's room and wait with her there."

Pepper led Katy through the double doors.

Next, Joshua waved Snake and Freddie over, "Do me a favor and go get Katy some breakfast. Bring her orange juice and coffee too."

The two nodded and took off. Joshua turned to the doctor, "Do you know what caused those puncture wounds?"

"I can't be sure."

"Doc, I'm not lookin' to sue you."

"I know you're not, Mr. Jacobs. After all, you paid for half of this hospital."

Joshua got quiet. When Sarah was sick, she received care there. Joshua didn't like the state of the facilities, so he made an anonymous donation, but the size of the donation made it impossible to protect his anonymity.

"What I meant to say is … the wound to your grandson's chest was most probably inflicted by a long-bladed knife that might have been serrated. As for the wound to his thigh, I can't be sure. It could have been shrapnel or broken glass … something irregularly shaped."

"Thank you, Doc."

Joshua walked to the lobby and took a newspaper from the stand. The headline read, "Escape from the Devil." Underneath the headline was a still photograph of a black-clad terrorist holding what looked like a serrated dagger to Josh's throat."

The bastard did try to kill Josh.

Joshua folded the paper under his arm and headed to Josh's room.

CHAPTER 14

DA'WAH OFFICE
FORMERLY CHURCH OF THE MARTYRS
AR-RAQQAH, SYRIA
NIGHT

Surrounded by his bodyguards and advisors, Shakir rested on a hospital bed brought to the former Church, now terrorist headquarters, especially for him. A doctor was listening to his heart with a stethoscope.

There was a knock at the door. A black-clad fighter entered and handed Shakir 8x10 photos and the NY Times newspaper. Shakir put the photos next to him and scanned the headline as his face filled with rage.

He pushed the doctor away, "Get out!"

As quickly as he could, the doctor packed his bag and left the room.

Shakir handed the newspaper to his advisors, "The American lives! The newspaper makes him sound like a hero and me, a buffoon!"

No one spoke as Shakir sat up staring straight ahead with fury in his eyes. After a minute, he picked up the photos. The first couple showed an SUV parked in a desert area. The next few were close-ups. Shakir recognized the man sitting in the driver's seat. He turned the photo to his advisors to be sure, "That is the U.S. border agent the Mexicans paid?"

His top advisor answered, "Yes, Shakir. His name is Herrera. He was warned not to spy on our people."

"Yet, there he is!" replied Shakir.

The advisor waited a moment to allow some of Shakir's anger to ebb, "I will contact the Mexicans and have them deal with him."

Shakir twisted his head to look at the newspaper in his advisor's hand, "Wait ... hand me the paper."

Shakir took the paper and looked at a smaller article under the main headline article. It read, "Hero returns to his Texas home-town." Next to the article was a photo of Josh in his dress blues and under it was a map showing Fort Stockton. Shakir thought for a moment, then picked up the 8x10s and thought for a while longer. He broke from his thoughts and snapped his fingers, "Show me where ... Fort Stockton, Texas is."

One of the younger advisors stepped forward with a small laptop. After typing in the location, he turned the laptop around to face Shakir.

Shakir motioned the advisor closer, holding up the photos, "Now, show me where these photos were taken."

The younger advisor conferred with the older and after typing the location, turned the laptop around again.

Shakir studied the two red markers on the map and grinned, "It appears my friend John Wayne ... what is the American saying ... has jumped out of the frying pan and into the fire, yes?"

His advisors looked confused.

Shakir waved for the laptop to be taken away, "First, get me something to eat then find out exactly where that American's mother lives. We have her address. And then contact our people in Paris. Tell them that I will be arriving there tomorrow, and tell them also that I want a French passport and identification papers made up for me to travel to Mexico."

The older advisor looked over at the younger before replying, "Shakir, with respect, it is not safe for you to travel so close to the United States. You never concealed your face. Even the people in Mexico could recognize you."

"I will take care of that."

"But Shakir—"

"Enough!" Shakir held his hand up, "The American made a fool of me to the world. He even drew my blood. Allah has been kind though. The map shows that we now have fifty fighters within striking distance."

Both advisors raised their brows. The older one spoke up again, "Shakir, those fighters were sent to carry out our first major assault on American territory. The operation took months to plan. We cannot risk their capture over an injured man and his mother. Our leaders and our financial supporters will not tolerate it."

Shakir tried to stare down his advisor, but the elder man didn't flinch. Shakir softened, "Our fighters will not be captured."

The advisor shook his hands, "How can you be sure of that?"

"Because I will be there to lead them."

Shocked, the advisor remained silent as a tray of food was placed over Shakir.

Shakir plucked a grape and placed it in his mouth, "Don't fear, my friend. I will fly to Mexico and cross into the United States the same way our fighters did. Then I will deal personally with the border agent before I pay a visit to my friend the cowboy and his mother. By the time you see pictures of their heads sitting on stakes I will already be back in Damascus."

Shakir sipped his coffee as he began writing on a sheet of paper, "And then, while the Americans are investigating their slayings, our fighters will be attacking their famous Alamo, hundreds of kilometers away."

Shakir put his pen down and handed the advisor the sheet of paper, "Have this mailed to the cowboy's mother."

The older advisor read the letter. It was written in English.

Katy Jacobs,

Your son cannot escape us. We will have his head and yours too. We know where you live.

We are coming.

He remained silent while blinking his eyes rapidly.

Shakir's expression turned cold, "I will have my revenge and the world will fear me more than ever."

CHAPTER 15

After showing his driver's license for identification, Joshua was waved through the checkpoint, pulling into Katy's driveway in one of the ranch pickups. He parked behind her truck, got out and scanned the street. It was filled with all sorts of official vehicles – police, FBI, DHS, DOD. A police chopper flew overhead as he was let into the house by two uniformed officers.

Inside, a dozen men, some dressed in uniforms, others in suits, stood around talking. Joshua recognized two of them. Border Patrol Agent Angel Martin was standing with Agent Herrera.

Agent Martin spotted Joshua and walked over offering his hand, "Hello, Mr. J."

Joshua shook his hand, "Where's my daughter-in-law?"

"She's in the kitchen speaking to the FBI. They're lead on this. It's a little crowded in there."

Joshua's eye met Herrera's, "What's he doing here?"

Martin put his hand on Joshua's chest, "Mr. J, no trouble, okay? You don't want to add to Katy's anguish, do you?"

"Tell him to take his corrupt ass-" Joshua brushed Martin's hand away, "Better yet, I'll tell him."

Herrera's hand disappeared into his jacket as Joshua approached him.

Joshua stepped nose-to-nose with Herrera and spoke softly, "You're not welcome here."

Martin grabbed Joshua's arms from behind, "Come on, Mr. J."

Joshua kept his eyes on Herrera, "I want you out of this house now."

Herrera noticed the men standing around were watching and listening. He pulled his hand from his jacket. It had the wallet with his bullet-dented badge in it. He flashed the badge at Joshua, "Whether I'm welcome or not, this gives me the authority to be here."

Herrera leaned towards Joshua and spoke into his ear, "We ain't in your country anymore."

A tall African-American man wearing a dark suit stepped out of the kitchen, "Agent Herrera, what's going on here?"

Katy appeared from behind him, "Joshua …?"

The tall man looked at Katy then to Joshua before nodding to Agent Martin, "Let go of him."

He offered his hand to Joshua, "I'm Special Agent Shivers, Mr. Jacobs. Would you follow me, please?"

Special Agent Shivers led Joshua and Katy into the kitchen. Herrera and Martin followed. Joshua glared at Herrera as he took a seat at the table next to Katy. Katy lit a cigarette.

Shivers took a sheet of paper from his attaché and placed it in front of Joshua, "Your daughter-in-law received this letter in the mail this morning."

Joshua read the letter.

Katy Jacobs,

Your son cannot escape us. We will have his head and yours too. We know where you live.

We are coming.

He looked up at Katy, who refrained from making eye contact.

Shivers took the letter back, "The letter was postmarked in Paris, but as you can see by the message, we believe it was sent by the same people that attacked Al Asad Air Base and took your grandson hostage."

Joshua jumped to his feet, "My grandson—"

Shivers held his hand up, palm out, "Mr. Jacobs, there's no need to worry, I have men guarding him. The police also have men patrolling near the hospital and Agent Herrera is monitoring the border."

Joshua glanced at Herrera, "I bet he is."

Shivers glanced at both men before continuing, "The police and my men will also be keeping an eye on this house. We'll have men stationed right outside."

Joshua looked down at Katy, "Katy, can I speak to you alone for a moment?"

Katy shook her head, "I know what you're gonna ask. The answer is no, Josh is not well enough to be moved."

"Hell, Katy, you know I could set your house on the ranch up with everything Josh needs. I'll hire nurses to stay with him round the clock—"

"That's not *my* house Joshua, and it ain't Josh's house either."

"Mr. Jacobs, your grandson and daughter-in-law are well-protected," added Shivers.

Joshua gave Herrera a long, cold stare, "Yeah … I see that."

He turned to Katy, "If you need anything …." He took a few steps then turned again, "Take care of my grandson, you hear."

Joshua walked out of the house and back to his pickup. He picked up his phone, "Pepper, it's me. Listen, I want you to send Snake to the hospital, and Freddie to Katy's house. Have 'em both stay out of sight. I want them to keep an eye out and to remain with them around the clock. If they have to be spelled, I want their best men to spell them, you hear?"

* * * * *

Across the street from Katy's house, a man stood at the window watching Joshua's truck pull away. Behind him, two other men were taping the mouths of the owners of the house, an elderly man and woman. The man at the window spoke into his satellite phone, in Arabic, "It looks like the authorities are beginning to leave. I will let you know when the time is right."

* * * * *

Shakir put his phone down. He was sitting in the passenger seat of a muddy Ford 4x4 turning onto the highway in front of the building with the red roof. He looked at himself in the side view mirror and smiled. His long, dark locks were slicked back and partially concealed by a Stetson and his eyes were concealed by aviator's sunglasses. He looked down at his clothes, a black leather jacket over a buttoned shirt, Wrangler jeans and black cowboy boots.

The driver looked at him and said in Arabic, "You look like a cowboy."

Shakir pulled his black-handled knife out and held it up, "I'm going to kill a cowboy."

CHAPTER 16

IRONMAN GYM
MARFA, TEXAS
AFTERNOON

Herrera opened his locker and smiled when he saw the gym bag lying inside. His smile disappeared when he lifted the bag. It was light, too light to have his payment in it. He opened it anyway. There was a typed note in it:

`You're being watched. There's a car waiting for you outside.`

Herrera reflexively scanned the locker room. He was alone. He slammed the locker shut, descended the stairs and saw a handful of people scattered about exercising. No one seemed to take notice of him. He walked near a window that looked out to the street and saw a dark sedan parked at the curb. He reread the note.

Who could be watching me …?

He rubbed his cheek.

Lozano knows if I end up dead or missing, so will he.

He crumbled the note and tossed it in the trash.

Time to get paid ….

Herrera walked out of the gym and got into the back of the

sedan.

* * * * *

Crouched down, Angel Martin watched as the car service sedan drove past him. He waited to allow a safe distance, and then took off after it.

CHAPTER 17

PECOS COUNTY MEMORIAL HOSPITAL
FORT STOCKTON, TEXAS
EVENING

Joshua approached Dr. Emerick outside of Josh's room. Joshua noted the tired smile on the doctor's face, and the bored sternness of the FBI agent stationed next to the door.

"Mr. Jacobs, your grandson is awake and the worst of it should be behind him."

Joshua's face flushed, "Thank you, Doc."

Dr. Emerick thumbed over his shoulder, "His mother is in with him. She looks like she hasn't slept in days."

"She hasn't. She's been going from the animal hospital to here and back to the animal hospital."

"Well, see if you can talk her into going home and getting some shut eye. She wouldn't take my advice."

"I will. When will Josh be released?"

"We'll run some more tests tomorrow. If all goes well, he'll be released tomorrow morning."

Joshua offered his hand, "Thanks again, Doc."

Joshua watched Dr. Emerick disappear around the corner before entering Josh's room. His entrance was met by two smiles – one slight one from Katy and a bigger one from his grandson. Katy was sitting in a chair she had pulled close to the bed, so she could hold her son's hand. Joshua thought she looked paler than Josh.

There was an I.V. in Josh's arm, but that didn't stop him from trying to sit up, "Gramps …."

Joshua removed his hat as he walked over to the bed. Tears welled as he rested his hand on his grandson's shoulder. He wiped them away as fast as he could but Katy noticed. Her smile made Joshua blush.

Joshua composed himself, "You put a scare into your mother and me. I got your letter."

Joshua ran his fingers through his hair, "I can't use a ranch hand … but we could use a Ranch Manager."

Josh tried to sit up taller, "Ranch Manager … that's Pepper's job."

"Pepper's getting old. It's getting time to put him out to pasture."

"Gramps …!"

"Not right away. You'll work at his side for a while. Besides, I ain't getting any younger. If you're gonna take over the ranch one day, you'll need to learn under Pepper first."

Josh's face lit up with joy, "What are we waiting for …." Josh started to get out of bed, but dizziness brought his head back to the pillow.

"Hold on there, the Doc said he wants to run a few more tests on you tomorrow before cutting you loose. The job will be there, meantime, get some rest."

Josh reached over with the I.V. arm and grabbed his grandfather's forearm, "Thank you, Grandpa … for everything."

Joshua nodded to him then turned to Katy, "It's time for you to go home and get some sleep, Dr. Emerick's orders."

Katy was about to protest when Joshua held up his index finger, "Now Katy, you ain't gonna make me hogtie and carry you outta here?"

Katy looked at Josh.

"You know he'll do it, Mama."

"I don't want to leave Josh alone."

Joshua walked over and put his hands on her shoulders, "I'm gonna run to the ranch to take care of a few things, but I'll be back here in an hour. Meantime, I'll have Snake sit with Josh until I get back. Now, come on, I'll drop you off at your house, on the way."

Katy stood up and gave her son a kiss on his cheek, "I could use a bath and a nap, but I'll be back here at sunrise. I love you, son."

"Love you too, Ma."

Joshua and Katy watched Josh close his eyes as they left the room.

* * * * *

Joshua escorted Katy to his pickup then walked over to Snake who was sitting in his own truck parked just outside the main entrance. The sky looked ominous and thunder could be heard in the distance.

Behind his truck was a dark sedan with government plates. Joshua eyed the man sitting behind the wheel wearing sunglasses then nodded to Snake in the direction of the car, "Looks like Agent Shivers kept his word."

"That is, if that one has his eyes opened behind those shades," replied Snake.

"I know. There's another one sitting outside Josh's room that looks bored to tears. Do me a favor … I gotta take care of a few things back at the ranch. Go sit in Josh's room until I get back, okay?"

"Sure thing. How's he doing?"

Joshua flashed a grin, "He's fine. Pepper's gonna have an assistant soon."

"About time! That ol' coot is getting crankier by the day."

Snake stepped out of the cab and started walking to the entrance. Joshua called out to him, "And Snake, why don't you buy the FBI some coffee ... to perk 'em up a bit."

Snake looked over at the one in the sedan who obviously heard Joshua's remark. Snake smiled and saluted with two fingers, "Will do!"

CHAPTER 18

ABANDONED WAREHOUSE
U.S. HIGHWAY 67, THREE MILES EAST
MARFA, TEXAS
EVENING

Herrera was apprehensive as the car pulled off the highway onto a dirt road. The driver turned up the radio to hear the weather report.

Dense fog has become widespread across Central, South, and Southeast Texas this evening, and it's definitely heading here to the Southwest. Moisture streaming northward ahead of our upcoming storm system, along with an inversion has caused widespread fog to form. This issue will continue tonight and into tomorrow morning.

The driver turned off the radio as Herrera looked ahead to an old warehouse that had seen better days. The car came to a stop in front of the building. The burly driver turned, "Get out."

Herrera's heart started beating faster. As soon as he closed the door, the car sped off leaving him choking on dust. Lightning lit up the horizon followed by a deep grumbling thunder.

Herrera was about to check his phone when out of the warehouse doors came six men all dressed in black, wearing balaclavas and armed with AK-47 assault rifles. They took positions on each side of Herrera. The two nearest him grabbed him by the arms and led him into the warehouse.

* * * * *

Agent Martin slowly rolled down the dirt path then turned off and drove a bit until he was about one hundred yards away from both the road and the abandoned warehouse. He watched as Herrera exited the car and it drove away.

Martin scanned the area through binoculars. He saw faint lights glowing from a few windows inside. Thunder echoed in the distance as fog began rolling over his truck.

* * * * *

Inside, the warehouse was mostly dark with small rays of light pouring in through the grimy windows. The armed men led Herrera down a corridor and past double doors into an immense empty space. The floors were concrete and painted, as if the space was once filled with machinery, but all Herrera could see was a small lit area towards the back.

He was escorted and made to sit in a metal folding chair. Four of the men then took positions nearby, behind the chair, while two stood with their rifles in hand, on the opposite side of a long table in front of him.

Herrera noticed maps of the Alamo on the table as he sat down. He heard the echoing of boot heels on the concrete floor. A man with long, dark locks and slicked back hair wearing a Stetson walked over. He was carrying a canvas sack slung over his shoulder.

The man placed the sack on the floor at Herrera's feet and leaned against the table. He was wearing aviator's sunglasses, even in the dim light.

Before Herrera could react, the men behind him grabbed his arms and held him down in the chair.

"Hey, what is this?! What the hell--?"

Shakir took his blade out and began to clean it with a cloth, "Do you know who I am?"

Herrera didn't reply. He was too distracted looking down at the blood leaking from underneath the sack.

"I'm the man that has been paying you."

"Lozano paid—"

"Lozano was hired to do a job. The money was mine." Shakir reached into the sack and pulled out Lozano's severed head. He held it by the hair and dangled it in front of Herrera's terrified face.

"Unfortunately for him, he did not give me value for my money. Instead, he gave me you."

Herrera shuddered, turning his head in revulsion, "Please, I did what I was told to do!"

"Did you? Were you not told to stay away from any of the crossing locations?"

Herrera blinked rapidly as all color left his cheeks, "I didn't—"

Shakir grabbed Herrera's hand and made him grasp Lozano's hair, "Don't let it go. Stare at it and consider what will happen if you lie to me."

Blood dripped from Lozano's severed neck as Herrera inadvertently shook it trying to hold it as far from him as he could, "No! I mean … yes, I went to the last crossing but only to make sure everything went well!"

"That was not your instruction."

Herrera was becoming frantic, "Do you know what you've

done?! Lozano was a Captain of the Zetas Cartel! Do you know who they are?!"

"I know who they are … infidels, like you. He deserved his death even before disappointing me." Shakir nodded to one of his men who picked up the canvas bag and returned Lozano's head to it, before taking it away. Herrera was still shaking as sweat dripped from his chin.

Shakir nodded to the rest of his men who let go of Herrera and stepped back into the darkness behind him. One of the men returned with a large tote bag. He set it down on the table next to Shakir. Shakir unzipped the bag and reached in. He pulled out wrapped bundles of hundred dollar bills, "Your pay.

"I'm a reasonable man. You were disobedient, but I will give you the opportunity to make amends."

Shakir ran his index finger along the back of his blade, "I want to know the locations of and the security arrangements for the American Marine Joshua Jacobs and his mother."

The sight of the money calmed Herrera some, but not entirely, "Why … why do you--?"

"My friend, you are not here to ask questions. You are here to answer them. Do this and you will get paid and go free." Shakir dropped the money back into the bag and zipped it.

Herrera wiped the sweat from his chin, "The kid is in the hospital in Fort Stockton. His mom is either with him or at the animal hospital where she works … or at her home."

"And their security arrangements?"

"The FBI has men watching them at the hospital and at her home. The police are also patrolling both areas."

Shakir nodded and one of his men came out of the darkness, took Herrera's phone from his pocket, and handed it to Shakir. Shakir handed it to Herrera, "You will call off those men."

Herrera took the phone, but shook his head, "I can't. They're not my men."

Shakir paused a moment then blinked his eyes. Once again, out of the darkness his men grabbed Herrera from the chair, forced him to his knees, and handcuffed his wrists behind him. Shakir grabbed Herrera by his hair and placed the serrated blade to his throat.

"Wait!! Wait! They're not my men, but I can do something!"

"What can you do?"

"The police force is small in Fort Stockton. I can have them all diverted to another part of town, at least for a short time … enough to allow you to get to the kid and his mom."

"But we don't know where his mother is, do we?"

"I can find that out!"

"What about the FBI? What can you do about them?"

"I can't … order them off—"

Shakir pulled Herrera's hair and pressed the blade into his throat.

"Wait!! I can point them out to you! I can even help you take them out! Please!"

Shakir let the blade linger on Herrera's throat before easing the pressure and slowly taking it away. As he did, his men took the handcuffs off and stood him up.

"First, you will make the phone calls and have the police diverted while on the way to the hospital with us."

Herrera started punching numbers then paused, "Diverted to where?"

"To here. I will leave a few of my men with enough firepower to pin them down here for a long time. Find out where the mother is while you are on the phone with them."

Lightning radiated every window as thunder shook the building.

Shakir looked out to see fog in the air. It put fire in his eyes, "The weather is on our side tonight."

Shakir raised his hands and grinned as his men looked on and smiled, "The Storm Demons have come to America."

Shakir walked off into the darkness as his men grabbed Herrera by his arms and followed. Herrera resisted until he saw one of them also grab the bag of money.

* * * * *

Agent Martin watched through binoculars as he saw Agent Herrera walk out of the abandoned warehouse. He was accompanied by seven other men. They poured into two SUVs and took off. He put the binoculars down and took off after them, careful not to follow too closely.

CHAPTER 19

KATY JACOBS RESIDENCE
ALPINE, TEXAS
NIGHT

Joshua pulled up into Katy's driveway and turned off the engine, "I'll wait here with you until Freddie gets here."

"That's really not necessary, Joshua," replied Katy as she exited the cab and headed for her door.

Joshua followed after her, "I think it is, at least for a while."

Katy unlocked the door and pushed it open, "And exactly how long is a while? Besides, I have the FBI watching the house and the police pass by all night long. It's not fair to the rest of the--"

Katy cut herself off when she saw Joshua looking off towards the street. Fog was in the air and it was being illuminated at times by lightning. The thunder seemed to come from every direction.

"What's the matter?"

Joshua scratched his chin, "I haven't seen any police since we left the hospital."

Katy looked down the street, "They'll be along. I'm sure. They've been around ever since Josh came back."

Joshua looked concerned. Katy pointed over his shoulder at a dark sedan parked across the street from her home, "You're forgetting my personal FBI bodyguard."

Katy waved at the man in the car. He waved back.

Katy swept her arm inviting Joshua in before closing and locking the door, "Honestly Joshua, I really don't know why everyone's making such a fuss about me, anyway. Josh is home and this is Texas, not Iraq."

Katy disappeared into the kitchen as Joshua stood in front of the window in the living room looking out at the FBI car parked on the street.

Katy called back to him, "You hungry? I'm starving."

Joshua gave the dark street one more scan before joining Katy in the kitchen, "I could use a bite. What do you have?"

Katy looked into the fridge and came out with a plate, "Leftover tamales," then reached back in and took out two bottles, "and two cold cervezas." She popped the tamales into the oven, twisted the tops off of the beer bottles, and handed one to Joshua.

Joshua clanked his bottle against hers, "To Josh."

Both took long pulls. "Thank God he's home and okay," added Katy.

They both sat down. Katy lit a cigarette with a familiar silver lighter.

"You know, you really gotta give them up," said Joshua, "they'll kill ya."

Katy shot him a wry look, "Your son James got me hooked. He liked to smoke when he drank," Katy smiled. She tossed Joshua the lighter, "That's his lighter. His company gave it to him for something or other."

Joshua looked at the inscription, "James Jacobs, Semper Fi."

They remained silent until Katy got up to fetch the tamales from the oven. Joshua broke the silence, "Katy, I want you to consider moving onto the ranch."

"And pass up this great cuisine?"

Joshua grinned, "That too, but that ain't why. You and Josh are my only family. I know we've had our differences over the years—"

"Is that what it was … differences?" Katy took another long pull from her bottle.

"Katy, I'm sorry."

Katy looked shocked hearing Joshua say those words.

"I'm sorry for a lot of things … for trying too hard to make you and James live on the ranch … and for my pigheadedness since then. I was wrong. But now young Josh wants to work the ranch and I intend to leave it to him when I'm gone."

Katy allowed a tired smile, "That's just fine, Joshua. I know it's what he wants and that's all that's important to me."

"But I want … I mean … I'd like it very much if you'd come to live on the ranch too." Joshua's eyes met Katy's, but she remained quiet. Joshua finally looked away, "I've missed Sarah."

Katy put her hand over Joshua's, "So have I."

He turned back to her, "She loved you as much as she loved James, you know." Joshua paused, "As do I."

Katy's lipped quivered hearing that as her eyes turned red, "Let me just walk this food to Mr. FBI out there, before the weather gets any worse."

Katy picked up a plate of tamales and headed out of the kitchen. Joshua took another pull from his beer as he watched the fog roll up onto the back of the house. He was about to finish what was in the bottle when he saw a shadow pass the kitchen window. In an instant, Joshua jumped up and ran after Katy, catching up to her a step away from the front door.

Joshua put his finger to his lips and spoke in a whisper, "Do you keep a gun in the house?"

It took a moment for Katy to reply, "A gun … yeah … yes, James's gun. It's upstairs in my bedroom in the drawer next to my bed."

Joshua grabbed her hand and led her up the stairs as voices could be heard outside the front door. Joshua locked them in her bedroom when they heard loud banging sounds followed by muffled voices coming from downstairs.

Joshua grabbed his son's Colt M45A1 pistol from the drawer, released the magazine to see that it was fully loaded, and then slapped the magazine back in and chambered a round. He used his finger to bend a blind so he could look out the window. There was no movement inside the FBI agent's sedan, and he see no one outside on the murky street.

Katy picked up the phone. She managed a nervous whisper, "The line is dead!"

They heard creaking coming from the stairs. Joshua put his finger to his lips again then pointed to the closet. Katy understood and got inside, while Joshua took a position with his back resting on the wall behind the door. Then he unlocked the doorknob.

Joshua watched as the doorknob turned and someone pushing the door open. He was cramped behind it. He waited until he saw the black figure of a man taking a step into the room. Then, in one motion, he stepped out and shot the man in the side of his head, while kicking the door closed, in the face of the man who was behind him.

Bullets immediately started chopping through the door. Within seconds the door burst open, the second man kicking it in and charging forward. The man sprayed part of the room with bullets before Joshua dropped him with three shots to his head. Once again, he kicked what was left of the door shut.

Joshua tucked James's pistol into the back of his jeans and picked up their rifles, then called Katy out of the closet and handed her one, "You point it and squeeze the trigger just like any rifle. Just don't hold down the trigger. Short bursts."

Joshua peeked out the window again. Dogs were barking and lights were turning on in nearby homes, but he still couldn't see anyone on the street. Before he could make a call, he and Katy heard voices speaking in Arabic outside the door.

Joshua pushed Katy onto the floor behind the bed and dropped to the floor himself as bullets started cutting through the remnants of the door. Wood splinters covered Joshua as the door was literally shredded. A third man dressed in black and wearing a black bala-clava like the first two, burst in with his rifle blazing.

Fortunately for Joshua and Katy, the man was aiming high. Joshua fired three quick rounds from the assault rifle into the man's throat. The man fell backwards into a fourth man behind him.

Joshua rolled behind the bed next to Katy as the fourth man opened up. Joshua returned fire until his rifle was out of ammo. He saw that the intruders were wearing harnesses with additional clips, but he couldn't reach any without exposing himself.

The sounds of a neighbor could be heard hollering outside, "Who the hell is shooting?" His hollering stopped when Joshua and Katy heard the sounds of automatic rifle fire.

Bullets continued to pour into the bedroom. Some of the rounds were chopping up the bed just inches from Joshua's head, pinning him to the floor. He motioned to Katy, pointing in the direction of the door.

Katy nodded then waited for a chance to rise up from behind the bed and emptied her entire magazine into the fourth man.

Joshua frowned at her, "I thought I told you short bursts!"

Joshua got up to try and make it to one of the corpses but saw a fifth man turning from the stairs and had to jump back behind the bed. Bullets followed him.

Joshua whispered to Katy, "Stay down, no matter what."

He waited for the gunfire to die down before taking one of the empty rifles and tossing it towards the door.

"Hey, we give up! Do you understand? We give up!"

A moment passed before a voice from the corridor replied in English, "Come out!"

Joshua showed his hands and kept them raised as he stood up. The man entered the room and looked around with his rifle pointed at him, "Where is the woman?"

"She's dead."

"Where is the body?"

Joshua lowered his left arm to point at Katy, while he swung his right arm behind his back to grab the pistol he tucked into the back of his pants, "She's right ... there!"

Joshua shot the man three times in his torso. The man fell back and hit the ground.

Katy sprung up from the noise.

"Get down!" Joshua shouted as the man rose up with his rifle bearing down on Katy. He emptied his last two shots into the fifth man's head.

Katy crawled to Joshua. He took her into his arms. As she wept, they heard creaking sounds from the stairs again. This time Joshua and Katy had no time to hide. The sixth man approached them, looking down at his fallen comrades. When he got to the threshold, he stopped and pointed his rifle.

Joshua held Katy as tightly as he could and turned away. The sound of the sixth man's body crashing to the floor followed after the sound of a Winchester rifle being fired. When he opened his eyes he saw Freddie standing at the top of the stairs aiming his rifle.

Joshua helped Katy to her feet and led her out of the room. He motioned to the rifle in Freddie's hands, "That mine?"

"It is. Mine is in my truck. I was standing by your truck when I heard shots, so I grabbed it."

Joshua handed Katy over to him, "Take her back to the ranch and wake everyone up." He headed down the stairs.

Freddie called after him, "Where are you going?"

Fog rolled into the house as Joshua opened the front door, "To the hospital, I'll meet you back at the ranch as soon as I get my grandson."

CHAPTER 20

PECOS COUNTY MEMORIAL HOSPITAL
FORT STOCKTON, TEXAS
NIGHT

Snake Vela, a proud Apache and Marine sat next to Josh Jacobs'
bed watching his favorite John Wayne movie, *Fort Apache*. The
Duke played Captain Yorke, while the great Henry Fonda portrayed
stuffy Lieutenant Colonel Thursday. Snake smiled and talked to
himself since young Josh was asleep, "I love this part!"

Lt. Col. Thursday: *I suggest the Apache had deteriorated since
then, judging by a few of the specimens I have seen on the way out
here.*

Captain Yorke: *Well, if you saw them, sir, they weren't Apaches.*
Snake pumped his fist, "Tell him, Duke!"

* * * * *

Sitting in the first of two SUVs were two fighters in the front
seats and Shakir and Herrera in the back. The SUVs were parked
out of the line of sight, around a turn behind the FBI vehicle. The
thickening fog and darkness of night also helped to conceal the

dark-colored trucks. Only the occasional lightning bolt illuminated them. Some drizzle had started to fall.

Herrera got off his cell phone. Shakir peered out the window in the direction of the sedan with the FBI agent inside, as he spoke to Herrera, "Is it done?"

Herrera nodded, "The police have all been diverted to the warehouse. They're setting up a perimeter since your people took shots at them. They should be pinned there for a while."

Shakir barely nodded, "That only leaves the FBI."

Herrera nodded again and pointed at the car, "Yes, one in that car and one guarding the room."

"And you can't order them away?"

"No."

"Then we will handle that ourselves," Shakir barked orders in Arabic.

Instantly, the two men sitting in the front seats got out and looked around before pulling balaclavas over their heads. No one was outside to see them as they made their way over to the FBI vehicle.

One went to the passenger side, while the second walked right up to the driver's door, pointing a pistol at the driver. Shakir and Herrera watched as both men entered the vehicle – one entered the front passenger seat while the pistol-pointing terrorist took a seat in the back.

Herrera and Shakir watched for over five minutes until curiosity prompted Herrera to ask, "What did you tell them?"

"I told them to make the one in the car contact the one guarding the door and tell him to come out to retrieve some food."

Herrera shook his head, "He won't leave his post."

Shakir grinned and pointed at the man exiting the hospital's front entrance, "Americans are so predictable."

They watched as the FBI agent approached the driver's side of the vehicle. The man in the backseat rolled down the window and pointed his pistol. Shakir and Herrera watched as the FBI agent got into the backseat. The engine was started and the car pulled away.

Herrera wondered where Shakir's men would take the two agents *… most probably somewhere dark and remote where they'd deliver a few bullets to their heads.*

Four men exited the second SUV and walked over to speak to Shakir.

"Stay here," Shakir ordered Herrera, as he exited the SUV. For a moment, Herrera thought of running, but memories of Lozano's severed head quickly changed his mind.

Shakir spoke to the men in Arabic before getting back in.

Two of the four immediately made a beeline for the main entrance, while the third disappeared into the darkness, and the fourth got into the driver's seat of their SUV.

Shakir turned to Herrera, "Now, you will go in there, flash your credentials, and tell them the Marine patient's location has been compromised and that a terrorist threat has just been confirmed against him. Tell them that he must be moved immediately, under your authority."

Herrera's eyes went wide, "I can't do that! Border Patrol doesn't have that kind of jurisdiction."

"Then you better fake it."

"It'll directly implicate me!"

Shakir remained devoid of emotion.

"I won't be of any more use to you if I do that! I'll be a fugitive!"

"Better a fugitive than a corpse," replied Shakir. "Go now. My men are waiting inside for you to give them the … how do you say

... all clear."

Herrera hesitated as sweat formed on his brow.

Shakir pulled out his serrated blade, "If even the thought of disobedience crosses your mind while inside, my men will bring you back to me, and I will do things to you that will cause you to beg to be beheaded."

"Can I ... disappear after I do it?"

"When the American is sitting next to me then I will give you your bag of money and you can disappear."

Herrera wiped the sweat from his forehead with the back of his hand then stepped out into the dense mist. He entered the lobby and stopped for a moment. He saw both of Shakir's men standing next to a soda machine with their eyes glued to him.

Herrera nodded once to them then marched up to the front desk. A solitary woman was sitting there reading a paperback novel. Herrera couldn't tell if she was a nurse or a clerk. He showed her his badge, "I'm Agent Herrera with the Border Patrol. Who's in charge here?"

* * * * *

Agent Martin sat and watched Agent Herrera follow two of the men from the abandoned warehouse into the hospital.

Josh Jacobs is in there! I better call--

He took his cell phone out only to see that a man standing outside the driver's door was pointing a pistol at him. The man waved him out of the truck and frisked him, taking away his phone, Glock, and identification before making him get in the back seat of the SUV that Herrera had just exited. He got in and sat next to a large man wearing a cowboy hat.

"Who are you?" asked Martin.

The man that led Martin over got in the front passenger's seat, handed Martin's identification to Shakir and pointed the pistol back at him. Shakir had his cell phone to his ear and a look of concern on his face as he examined the I.D.

After a moment, Shakir shoved the phone into his pocket and spoke in Arabic to his men, "No one is answering at the mother's house."

Neither man replied or showed any emotion.

Shakir handed Martin back his I.D. and switched to English, "You are with the Border Patrol. Do you work with Agent Herrera?"

Martin put his I.D. away, "I work with Herrera. Know him?"

Shakir glanced at his men who continued to remain stoic. Shakir ignored the question, "Why were you following us?"

Martin ignored his, "I already reported this to Border Patrol. If I were you, I'd let me out and scram before they get here."

Shakir initiated a hardened stare at Martin who returned, in kind. Shakir took his cell phone and made a call, "What is the status?"

Herrera answered his phone, "They bought it. They're sending a nurse to his room to prepare him for transport. Your men are about to head to his room."

Shakir looked at his watch, "We must move quickly. I'm sitting here with an Agent Martin, do you know him?"

Herrera turned his back on the lady at the front desk, "Martin ... what is he doing here?"

"He was following us. I'm not sure from where. He said he reported our presence here to Border Patrol. Can you check?"

"Give me a minute," Herrera placed Shakir on hold and made another call, "It's Herrera, has Martin called in recently ... no ... no, no message for him. Thanks."

Herrera got back on with Shakir, "He didn't call anyone at Border Patrol."

"Very well, you must hurry," Shakir put his cell phone away and turned to Martin, "You will learn very soon the penalty for lying to me. For now, sit and remain quiet."

Martin rubbed the sweat from his palms onto his thighs, as he tried to make out the main entrance through the growing fog.

CHAPTER 21

PECOS COUNTY MEMORIAL HOSPITAL
FORT STOCKTON, TEXAS
NIGHT

After hearing sounds of gunfire, Josh Jacobs opened his eyes to
see the sounds were coming from the TV, a fight between Apaches
and the U.S. Cavalry. He looked next to him, "Uncle Snake, when
did you get here?"

Snake jumped to his feet, "Your grandpa wanted me to sit with
you while he took care of a few things. How are you feeling, Josh?"

"I feel like a mule kicked me in the side of my head ... and I'm
starving."

"I'm hungry too. I'll see if the cafeteria is still open."

"Forget about the cafeteria. You know what I want ... I could go
for a Toro Burger!"

"I ain't driving all the way to El Paso, jefe, but there's a Mickey
D's down the road." Snake headed for the door.

Josh's laughter was laced with pain, "I guess that'll have to do ...
a Big Mac and large fries ... and don't forget an apple pie."

Snake stepped into the corridor and noticed the empty chair
where the FBI agent should have been sitting. He looked both ways.

The corridor was empty and quiet.

He headed to the lobby and approached the front desk, where a man was standing there. He appeared to be waiting for a response from the woman seated behind the counter. As he approached the counter, two dark-haired men passed him.

Snake thumbed over his shoulder and spoke to the woman, "Excuse me … there is supposed to be an FBI agent on guard in front of Josh Jacob's room. Do you know where he went?"

The woman looked at the man standing next to Snake. Snake could sense that the man was nervous.

"I'm Agent Herrera with the Border Patrol. And you are?"

"Border Patrol, why are *you* here?"

Herrera noticed that the lady behind the desk was listening to their conversation, "I asked you your name."

"Snake Vela, I work for Joshua Jacobs. I'm visiting his grandson."

Herrera concealed his concern, "Well, we're about to transfer Mr. Jacobs' grandson to another hospital. His security has been compromised here. The FBI agents guarding him are already scouting the new location."

Snake raised a brow, "What hospital are you taking him to?"

"I'm afraid I can't tell you that."

Snake took his cell phone out. Herrera snatched it from him, "Sir, I'm afraid you also can't make any phone calls right now, at least until Mr. Jacobs' son is in transit."

"I was going to call Mr. Jacobs."

"Mr. Jacobs will be notified as soon as his grandson is secured at the new location."

Snake kept his eyes on Herrera as he started for the door. Herrera grabbed him by his arm, "I also can't allow you to leave until we are on our way."

Snake noticed Herrera's empty holster and pulled his arm free, "I'd like to see you try to stop me."

Herrera cursed to himself. He made a call as Snake walked out the main entrance, "The man that just walked out needs to be stopped!"

Shakir put his phone down and ordered the driver in Arabic. The driver immediately took out his pistol, exited the SUV, and headed for Snake.

* * * * *

Snake exited the hospital and began walking at a fast clip to his truck. Through the thickening mist, he spotted the silhouette of a man walking towards him. The fog didn't conceal the pistol in the man's hand, and Snake didn't give away that he seen it.

Snake knew he couldn't make it all the way to his truck by the time the man would get close enough to spring into action. He was armed with a knife but decided against using it.

I can't be sure if that dude's with Border Patrol or some other agency. But none of this feels right!

Snake reached the end of the building and quickly turned the corner. Shakir's man was still several paces behind him. As he reached the corner, Shakir's man was greeted by Snake's hand yanking the barrel of his pistol.

* * * * *

Shakir and Martin watched as both Snake and Shakir's man disappeared around the corner of the building. They were parked too far away to see or hear anything.

Infuriated, Shakir barked orders in Arabic to the man in the passenger seat. Instantly, the man jumped out of the SUV with pistol in hand and began jogging in the direction of where both men disappeared.

Shakir pulled his pistol and kept it low and pointed at Martin, "Do you know that man?"

Martin shrugged and shook his head, "It's so foggy out there I couldn't see."

Martin could tell that the man holding the gun on him was uneasy.

This shit ain't going the way el jefe planned.

* * * * *

A middle-aged nurse walked into Josh's room, headed over to his I.V., and removed it.

Josh smiled, "Thank you ma'am that was starting to annoy me."

The nurse smiled and walked over to the closet. She began taking Josh's clothes and laying them on a chair, as two men dressed in black walked in and stared at her. Josh noticed they avoided eye contact with him.

"More company … who are you guys?"

The nurse waited for them to answer before answering herself, "They're here to transport you to another hospital."

Josh sat up, "Another hospital? Why?"

The nurse waited for either of the two to respond before replying again, "You'll have to ask them." She turned to the men, "I'll be back with a wheelchair."

The nurse left the two men alone in the room with Josh.

He didn't like the look of them, but acted casual, "You boys hungry? I was waiting for a friend to bring me back some McDonald's. I'm starving."

Neither man replied. They remained staring blankly at him, with their arms folded in front of them. Josh noticed the bulges of pistols under their jackets.

The nurse walked back in pushing a wheelchair. Josh noticed both men reach for their weapons out of reflex. The nurse didn't notice, tossing a bag from the closet onto the chair with his clothes, and then locking the wheelchair in place next to the bed.

Next, she fetched hospital slippers from the closet and dropped them to the floor, next to the wheelchair.

With a smile, she pulled Josh's covers down, "Think you can stand up on your own and get yourself in the wheelchair?"

With a glance at the men, Josh threw his legs over the side of the bed, "I think I can handle that, ma'am. Can I ask a favor? Would you mind contacting my mother for me?"

The nurse looked again at the two men before shaking her head in frustration, "I think these gentlemen and their boss are handling that for you."

Josh kept his eyes on the men as he stood up and slipped his feet into the slippers. He noticed how neither offered to help him as he took a seat in the wheelchair.

In a practiced motion, the nurse stepped behind him, undid the wheel lock, and pushed him over to the men, "He's all yours."

Without even a nod of reply, Shakir's men waited for the nurse to leave before one got behind Josh's wheelchair and started pushing him out of the room, while the other held the door open.

Josh noticed the empty chair outside his room where the FBI agent would have been sitting. The agent was nowhere in sight. His mind began racing.

Who are these guys? Is it my imagination or do they look Middle Eastern ... and they're dressed in black ... here in Texas?

From the corner of his eye, Josh noticed Snake emerge at the end of the corridor. Snake looked right at him and nonchalantly shook his head, prompting Josh to kick the footrests closed and grip the armrests.

That was Snake's cue. He raced down the corridor to get behind the two, pointing the pistol he took and hollered, "No one move!"

Cringing from pain, Josh jumped up when he saw both men reaching for their pistols. With a loud grunt, he kicked the wheelchair into them sending their aims wide. Their shots pierced the ceiling and wall at almost the same moment Snake's pierced their foreheads. Both bodies hit the floor with a thud.

Within seconds an alarm went off.

Without hesitation, Snake quickly picked up the men's weapons and handed one to Josh, "Can you walk?"

Josh worked the slide, "I'll do the Texas Two-step with y'all if you tell me what the hell is going on?"

Snake led the way jogging down the corridor, "I don't know, but one thing's for sure ... they ain't with the Border Patrol."

Josh struggled to keep up, "The Border Patrol ...?"

Snake rounded the corner, "I'll tell you about it later. Right now, we'll use the back doors and try to make it to my truck."

"What then?"

"Your granddad should be getting back here any time now."

* * * * *

Shakir's anger grew stronger as his patience wore thin. Enraged, he flashed his teeth as he put the phone to his ear, "What is taking so long!"

Still inside the lobby, Herrera held his finger in one ear to muffle the blare of the alarm as he stared down the corridor. He saw no one.

He shouted his reply, "I don't know. But shots just rang out from somewhere inside the hospital."

"Find out!" Shakir shoved the phone back into his pocket.

Martin grinned, "Problems?"

Shakir snarled as his phone rang. He answered it keeping his eyes firmly on Martin's. It was his man at the corner of the building, speaking Arabic, "I found Emir. He was knocked unconscious."

Shakir lips quivered as he failed to keep his voice in check, "Where is the man who walked out?"

"I do not know. He is not here. Shakir, he took Emir's gun."

"Check the parking lot!" Shakir disconnected the call.

* * * * *

Snake scanned the gloomy parking lot before waving Josh to follow him. Patches of dense fog draped to the ground in both directions, only separated by patches of mist. The two made it all the way to Snake's truck, but not before Shakir's men appeared from behind a parked car. One was pointing his gun directly at Josh, "Drop your weapons."

Snake and Josh complied. The second man ran over and took back his own pistol, before tucking the other one into his belt.

The one named whom Snake had knocked unconscious stabbed his pistol into Josh's back and pointed ahead, "Walk."

Snake and Josh took only one step before a rifle shot rang out from somewhere. They turned to see the first man crumble to the ground.

Snake wasted no time pulling the knife he kept concealed in his belt buckle and slamming it into the neck of the second man. He watched as life left his eyes.

Snake and Josh scanned the lot. Out of one of the pockets of mist came Joshua, carrying his rifle over his shoulder, "Good evening, gentlemen … Josh, glad to see you up and around."

"Gramps …! What the hell is going on?"

Joshua motioned to Snake's truck, "Uncle Snake will take you to the ranch. I'll catch up to you."

Snake and Joshua helped Josh into Snake's truck. Snake rolled down the window, "Joshua, where the hell are the cops and FBI?"

"I don't know, but whoever did this attacked Katy's house too. That's where I came from."

"My mom …? Josh hollered.

"She's okay. I had Freddie run her back to the ranch. It looks like your enemies followed you home, Josh."

"Joshua, that one from the Border Patrol … Herrera, he's here and he has to be in on whatever is going on. He was inside the lobby and gave me some cock-and-bull story about how Josh had to be moved to another hospital."

Joshua's upper lip curled at the mention of Agent Herrera's name. He banged on the door, "Get Josh out of here. There might not be much time, but try to alert everyone on the ranch. This ain't over."

Josh leaned forward, "Take care of yourself, Grandpa."

"Take care of yourself and your Mama."

Joshua watched the truck disappear into the fog then started for the back door of the hospital, as lightning lit up patches all around, and thunder rumbled shaking the ground.

* * * * *

Herrera entered the corridor and saw the bodies of Shakir's men lying in pools of their own blood behind an empty wheelchair. He heard muffled screams as nurses and patients were peeking out from their rooms along both sides of the hallway.

He checked the bodies for life then looked into Josh's room before calling Shakir, "The kid is gone and your men are dead."

"Gone … where could he go?!"

"Did you stop the man I told you to?"

Shakir looked at Martin with a hint of embarrassment, "My men … haven't reported in yet."

"Well, he probably was responsible for this. He works for Joshua Jacobs, the boy's granddad."

"Where could they be heading?"

"They're probably on the way to Joshua's Country. That's—"

Joshua appeared at the end of the corridor pointing his rifle at Herrera. Herrera lifted his hands into the air with the phone still in his hand, "I'm unarmed."

Joshua approached him with caution, "Are you responsible for all this?"

"I had no choice. He made me bring them here."

"Who made you?"

"Someone who wants your grandson dead, badly."

Joshua saw Herrera's phone. He held his hand out. Herrera handed him the phone. Joshua put it to his ear, "Are you the one after my grandson?"

* * * * *

Shakir pulled the phone from his ear briefly in disbelief.

* * * * *

"Cat got your tongue? Well, listen up. This ain't the Middle East and it ain't Paris. This is Texas, boy. We shoot back here."

Joshua tucked the phone into his pocket and poked Herrera in the chest with the barrel of his rifle, "So you told them where my daughter-in-law lived, sent the police on a fool's errand ... and led these men right to my grandson."

"I told you ... I had no choice."

Joshua stepped over the corpses, "Well, now you're gonna lead me to them."

Herrera shook his head, "Listen to me. The leader is a mad man. He's sitting in the back seat of an SUV out there and he's armed. He has a gun on Agent Martin right now and he has other men here. We can't go out there."

"We can't, but you can."

Joshua thought a moment then motioned with his rifle at a large green oxygen tank on a wheeled stand, "Check if that tank is full."

Herrera returned a confused look as he examined the gauge, "It's full, why?"

"You're gonna wheel it out the main entrance."

Herrera hesitated. Joshua cocked his Winchester, "You do what I tell you or I'll fill you with so many holes, you'll beg me to put you down."

Herrera shook from fear, "You'll just kill me, anyway!"

"You wheel that tank right up to the back door of that SUV then run like hell. I'll give you five seconds to run and duck."

"Five seconds ... that ain't enough!"

Joshua aimed the rifle at Herrera's head, "It's five seconds more than I'll give you, if you don't do it."

* * * * *

Shakir's eyes became wild with fury. The American's grandfather just threatened him and hung up. He shook from anger and something else ... something he wasn't used to feeling ... fear.

He pressed the barrel of his pistol against Martin's temple, "Answer me or you will die ... where is ... Joshua's Country?"

Even with a gun pressed to his head, Martin had to smile, "I can take you there if you'd like, but you better say your peace to Allah first."

Shakir snickered, "You talk like this man is to be feared," he tapped the barrel against Martin's temple, "I am the one to be feared! I will cut off his son's head in front of him and then—"

Lightning lit up the cloud of fog all around the SUV accompanied by thunder so powerful it rocked the vehicle. In the lightning's glow, Shakir saw a figure approaching wheeling some sort of cart. Martin turned to see what it was. He answered the question without thinking, "Herrera ...."

Shakir pressed the pistol against Martin's head again, "What is that with him?"

Martin took a moment, "I don't know. It looks like ... a tank."

"A tank ...?"

Shakir tried to make sense of the confusion as he watched Herrera wheel the tank closer. He and Martin could see the look of terror on Herrera's face.

Herrera cried out as he approached the front of the truck, "I did what you said! Please … don't shoot!"

Shakir thought aloud as he gazed out, perplexed at Herrera, "Has the infidel lost his mind? Why would I shoot him if—"

Herrera stopped pushing the tank. He looked over his shoulder in terror.

Martin cowered next to Shakir, covering his head with his arms, "He's not talking to you!"

Herrera took a step to run.

Confused, Shakir ducked down on top of Martin as they both heard a rifle report.

The ground shook from the force of the explosion even more so than from the thunder.

All the windows of the SUV blew out as the vehicle was pelted with metal fragments from the giant fireball where Herrera and the oxygen tank had been.

Shakir's back was covered with glass and debris. Martin wasted no time pushing Shakir off him and rolling out of the wrecked vehicle. It took a little longer to get his bearings before Shakir also rolled out and took off running into the fog.

Joshua appeared from the flames pointing his rifle. He looked around, "Angel, you alive?"

The reply came from somewhere to his left, "Barely. Damn, Mr. J, you could've killed me!"

Joshua made his way over to Martin while still scanning the area with his rifle, "I would've … killed that son of a bitch, but Herrera stopped too far away."

The two spotted Herrera's body lying face down on the ground. Martin looked at Joshua sternly, "You lit Herrera up pretty badly, Mr. J."

"Yeah, well, he deserved it."

Martin wiped the soot from his jacket, "I reckon he did."

"Any idea where that old boy went?"

"He's heading to your ranch. He got a call then he asked me about Joshua's Country."

"Damn. That was Herrera's last sin."

"I didn't tell him where it was, but I figure it won't take him long to figure it out."

Joshua started walking briskly as the sound of police sirens could be heard in the distance. Martin called after him, "Mr. J, where are you going? You gotta stay here and explain what happened!"

Joshua replied without turning around, "You can explain. When Shivers gets here, tell him to move his ass!"

Martin watched as Joshua got in his truck and drove away.

CHAPTER 22

THE DOUBLE-J RANCH – MAIN GATE
PECOS COUNTY, TEXAS
PRE-DAWN

The rain had stopped, but there was no moon. Because the fog was so thick, Joaquin was only standing a few feet away, but he could only hear the large main gates being forced open.

Joaquin remained totally undetected to the intruders as he counted six sets of headlights roar past him.

Grabbing the reins, he remounted his pinto while speaking into a walkie-talkie, "It's Joaquin. The uninvited have just arrived, six vehicles heading for the hacienda."

Joshua's voice crackled from the radio, "Snake, your braves in position?"

* * * * *

"Si, jefe," replied Snake from a treed area near the path to the hacienda.

"Remember, I don't want any of our people hurt. Strike and disappear."

"That's the Apache way, jefe."

* * * * *

"Okay, Joaquin, lock 'em in and don't open that gate for no one except the federalis. They should be led by a man named Shivers."

"Si, jefe."

Joaquin rode over to a small panel built into the side of the guard shack and punched in a security code, which unlocked a small hood covering a switch. He pressed the switch, and from the ground where the main gates had been, a thick iron wall arose. It ascended as high as the ranch's twelve-foot brick perimeter walls.

Joaquin rode up to the metal barricade and knocked on it with his knuckles, "No one's getting out of here."

* * * * *

Still miles from Joshua's hacienda, the terrorist convoy had to slow down. Though mostly traveling straight, up to that point, the dirt road began swerving left and right around trees and gullies. Twice, the lead SUV had skid to a halt, almost hitting a tree the first time, and almost driving down into a gully, the second.

Shakir's impatience erupted when they came to a complete stop. He grabbed his walkie-talkie and shouted, "Why have we stopped?!"

The lead driver responded, "There are animals blocking the road."

Shakir and his men jumped out of their SUV and walked rapidly to the lead vehicle. All the men were dressed in their familiar black clothing and balaclavas. As always, Shakir's clothes matched theirs, but his head was exposed.

They began hearing mooing coming from the mist in front of them. He turned the spotlight on bolted to the driver's door.

Shakir motioned to the lead driver, "You and your men go check to see how to get around the animals."

Seven men from the lead SUV jumped out and began heading down the dirt road, pointing their rifles in all directions.

Shakir turned around and spoke into his walkie-talkie, "I want everyone out of the vehicles and on guard, until we can get moving again."

Shakir couldn't see anyone, but he could hear doors opening and closing behind him. He and his men were comfortable operating inside the dark cloud. They were, after all the "Storm Demons."

Shakir checked a map on his cell phone then spoke to the men standing around him, "We are only two kilometers from the big house. The American Marine and his mother will be there along with this Joshua."

One of the men from the lead SUV returned from the mist, "Shakir, the cows are scattered all over the road for many meters. We can pass them through the trees to the left, but the trucks cannot fit through."

Startling them, gunshots began popping off from somewhere, a combination of AK-47 and some other kind of rifle reports. Shakir had never heard that kind of rifle. He yelled into his walkie-talkie, "What is going on?!"

No one replied.

The gunfire continued for awhile longer then petered out.

Shakir tried again, "I want a report! What is going on? Who is shooting?"

Someone finally replied, "Shakir, come to the rear truck!"

Shakir and the men from his SUV took off running. They reached the rear vehicle only to find all the men around it dead from gunshot wounds.

Shakir checked some of the bodies and saw that many of the kill shots were deadly accurate, striking his men in their heads. He looked up at the fighter who reported, with fury in his eyes, "Who did this?"

The fighter pointed out into the pitch-dark gloom, "The shots came from that direction, but when we reached the tree line, no one was there."

Shakir strained to look, "They must be on foot. They could not drive vehicles in that direction. Take your men, find and kill them!"

Six more of Shakir's men ran off following the one he ordered and disappeared into the trees.

Shakir spoke into his walkie-talkie, "Everyone, meet up with me ahead of the lead truck. We must go on foot from here. I want a lead team to take the point and another to cover our rear."

* * * * *

Snake Vela and his dozen Apaches watched Shakir and his men walk off from the side of the path opposite the tree line.

He took his radio out, "It's Snake. We took out seven of them and another six set off in the direction of the pastures."

Joshua's voice broke through, "Anyone hurt?"

"Just dead."

"Good work."

"You want us to tail the main body? They're heading your way on foot with the big ugly one leading them."

"Negative. Take off after the six heading for the pastures. See if you can sneak up on them."

Snake chuckled along with his men, "We're Apaches Joshua. That's the only way we operate."

Snake put his radio away and started in the direction of the tree line with a dozen Apaches following him.

Shakir checked the map on his phone then radioed to his men, "We are about a half-kilometer from the house."

He looked down at his boots to see that the fog was beginning to dissipate. The voice of one of his men from the squad on point came from his radio, "Shakir, we found something."

Shakir looked out ahead of him and replied into his radio, "What is it?"

"It looks like a big round hat. It is lying in the middle of the road."

"Do not go near it! Move off the road and go around it. High alert … it could be a trap."

The leader of the point squad obeyed Shakir and headed off of the dirt path with his men in tow down a shallow embankment. They stopped and gathered around the leader when he saw something.

The leader, a bright but young radical radioed Shakir, "Shakir, there is a box on the ground. I thought it might be an IED, but I have never seen anything like it. Perhaps it is some sort of motion detector. There is English writing on it."

Shakir looked out in their direction, in the distance, and radioed back, "What does it say?"

"I cannot read English."

* * * * *

Shakir cursed to himself, "Use your camera and show me."

Shakir looked at his phone as the men from the squad on point became visible. Very quickly, the camera view switched from them to a rectangle box lying on a slight angle, on its side. Shakir's eyes opened wide when he saw what was written on it – FRONT TO-WARD ENEMY.

Shakir hollered into his radio, "GET AWAY!"

Everyone ducked from the deafening blast and flash of light bursting out from the lead squad's position.

Shakir and the rest of his men ran to the spot of the explosion. While his men took up guard positions, Shakir looked down from the path to see all the men of the lead squad lying dead. Their bodies were riddled with gaping wounds caused by the steel balls projected from the M18A1 Claymore mine that had just exploded.

* * * * *

One hundred meters away, lying on his back, Freddie Gonzalez rolled over and spoke into his radio, "One of the Claymore's did its job, Joshua, but I only had two positioned on each side, and they look like they are sticking to the path now. There are many still heading your way."

"You did fine, Freddie, now get back to your house and guard your family."

"Si ... Joshua, take care of your family and yourself."

Freddie got to his feet and ran off into the darkness.

CHAPTER 23

THE DOUBLE-J RANCH – JOSHUA JACOBS HACIENDA
PECOS COUNTY, TEXAS
DAWN

Joshua peered out of the living room window of his home and saw the thick fog from the night before becoming a rolling mist, as dawn approached.

Joshua watched as Pepper's truck pulled up behind Joshua's and Freddie's trucks, about fifty feet from the front door.

Joshua turned to Josh and Katy, "Pepper's here." He spoke into his radio, "Joaquin, any sign of the cavalry?"

Sitting on a couch, young Josh and Katy stared at him waiting for the reply. A moment passed before it came, a single word, "Negative."

Joshua returned their stare as he replied, "Understood. When they get there, you make sure they hightail it to my hacienda, comprende?"

"Si, jefe, I'll lead them there myself."

Joshua took down an identical Winchester to his, from the wall-mounted gun rack. He handed it to his grandson, along with boxes of cartridges, "Take your mom into the closet in the kitchen. It's the most centered room in the house."

Katy helped her son to his feet, and after steadying himself, he cocked the rifle, "I ain't sitting this out in a closet, Gramps. We're both Marines."

Joshua's eyes sparkled with pride, but his heart was filled with fear, "Well, your mama isn't, Katy, get yourself—"

Katy walked to the gun rack and took down another identical Winchester rifle. She cocked it like she saw her son do, "I'm the mother of a Marine and I ain't sitting this out either."

Joshua nodded to Katy as his radio crackled to life. It was Pepper, "Joshua, I hear noise coming from the path."

Joshua looked out the window again, "Do you see anyone?"

"Negative ... wait—"

The sound of automatic rifle fire erupted.

Joshua ducked and shouted into his radio as Josh joined him on the opposite side of the large window, "Pepper, move your ass!"

Pepper didn't reply. The old drill sergeant stood firing his rifle several times, in the direction of the path, before turning and running for the front door of the hacienda.

Inside, Joshua ran to the front door, opened it and began firing over Pepper's head to lay down cover.

Pepper made it as far as the porch before a bullet slammed into his back. He collapsed on the steps.

"Pepper ...!" Joshua hollered as he stuck his head out the door, only to be driven back by a hail of bullets. With tears forming, Joshua was forced to close and lock the door, before returning to the window in the living room.

"Where's Pepper?" asked Josh.

Joshua looked first at Josh then to Katy, "He took a round to his back. I couldn't get to him."

Katy had been kneeling behind her son. She stood up in front of the window, "We can't just leave him out there … he could be alive!"

Glass from the window suddenly flew in all directions as bullets sprayed into the room. Joshua tackled Katy and laid over her until the rifle fire was silenced by young Josh's return fire.

Joshua pointed, "Katy, get in the fireplace and keep a watch on the entry to this room. Shoot anyone you see."

Katy looked at Joshua with tears of her own. She leaned up and kissed him on the cheek, "Thank you for saving my son and me. You can be as stubborn as a mule … but you're a good man, Joshua."

"The Good Book says, no man is good, except one … and that ain't me. Now get!"

Katy smiled then crawled and took a position in the giant stone fireplace. Joshua watched as she followed his instructions, pointing her rifle at the room's entryway. He flashed a momentary grin before rifle fire pulled him back to the activity outside.

Josh fired his rifle then looked over at his grandfather, "They're fanning out. From what I could see, they have enough men to surround the house and keep us pinned down."

"They don't want to keep us pinned down. That big one came all the way here to kill you. Damn if you didn't piss him off, Josh."

Josh grinned, "I don't think he likes Texans, Gramps."

Joshua's brows drew in as he scowled, "Is that a fact."

Joshua cocked his rifle, took aim and downed one of the terrorists running for the side of the house.

"Well, I'm done playin' with this ugly, American-hating, beheading son-of-a-bitch …," Joshua cocked, fired and downed another terrorist running for the opposite side of the house.

As the report of that last shot died out, it became dead silent outside the house, followed by a deep voice bellowing something in Arabic. The same voice then shouted in English, "You inside the house. I will only make this offer once. Throw your weapons out and walk out the door, and I will spare the woman."

Joshua glanced from Josh to Katy. Both of them returned stern looks of defiance. He shouted in reply, "Go to hell!"

The same voice bellowed another order in Arabic. This time, from out of the mist stepped the black-clothed and masked men surrounding the house, each with a rifle in hand.

On cue, they released a deluge of automatic rifle fire that tore into the hacienda from all sides, shredding walls and picture frames, including a portrait of Sarah that hung over the fireplace. The torrent lasted for over a full minute before everything returned to silence.

Shakir shouted, "Since you will not come out, I will come in and behead your grandson in front of his mother. Then I will set you both on fire."

Shakir barked orders and once again his men opened up on all sides of the house, except for two men who walked ahead of him to the front door. Not paying it any mind, the two men walked over Pepper's body and up the porch stairs. They aimed their rifles at the doorknob and riddled it with bullets until the door flung open.

Shakir stepped over Pepper's body and headed up the wooden stairs. He made it as far as the doorway when he was knocked to the ground from two bullets slamming into his back.

His men turned to see a bloodied Pepper on his knees pointing a rifle at them. Pepper fired at them but missed, as they ducked to each side of the door before closing it.

Pepper struggled to get to his feet. Realizing the gunfire from all around the house had ceased again, he turned around, using his rifle as a crutch. Before him stood a dozen terrorists with their rifles trained on him.

Before any of them could pull the trigger, shots suddenly rang out dropping two of them. Pepper looked beyond them to see Snake and his Apaches galloping out of the pasture. He collapsed to his knees grinning, "Never turn your back on an Apache."

* * * * *

Shakir's men helped him to his feet. The two bullets Pepper fired were still lodged in the back of his bulletproof vest. Shakir grimaced in pain, "I should kill you both for not checking to see if that one was dead!"

Shakir's radio came alive, "Shakir, men on horses rode up behind us. We were able to drive them back, but more could be on the way. Daylight has come and the fog is lifting. We must leave now."

Shakir looked at the men in front of him with rage before replying, "Do not tell me what I must do! I know what I must do. Everyone, prepare to storm this house on my command!"

Shakir waited for a reply. After a pause, it came, "On your command."

* * * * *

Joshua reloaded his rifle while keeping an eye out the window. He snapped his fingers at Josh who had taken a position near Katy, "I should've known that bad-tempered old man wouldn't go that easy." Joshua added under his breath, "Thank you, Pepper."

Joshua scanned from left to right down his rifle's site, "Snake and the Apaches drew their fire away from the house, but something's changed. They're looking our way again."

Josh pointed in the direction of the foyer, "They're in the house."

Joshua crawled over to his grandson and Katy and knelt on one knee between them, "They're coming ... all of them. Kneel down next to me."

Katy and Josh did as he said.

"There's only two ways into this room – the entryway and the window. Josh, you keep your rifle on the window. Shoot 'em as they climb in. Katy, you keep yours on the entryway. I'll shoot the ones that make it in here."

"Joshua," Pepper's voice came through Joshua's radio.

Joshua grinned, "Pepper, you ol' son-of-a-bitch, I thought you were too ornery to be put down. Where are you?"

"Thanks to Snake and them damn Indians. Never mind where I am. Listen to me. They're coming."

"Tell me something I don't know."

"The big ugly one, I shot him in the back, but I think he's wearing a vest. He's inside the house and has friends."

"Are you gonna tell me something I don't know?"

There was a short pause.

"On her deathbed, I told Sarah I'd keep an eye on you and Katy."

Joshua glanced at Katy. Tears fell from her eyes.

"I'm too shot up to do that, now. So, you're gonna have to look out for one another from now on."

Joshua gazed up at the shot-up portrait of Sarah.

"You hold on, you ol' son-of-a-bitch. You hear me?"

There was no reply.

Joshua's eyes blazed, "Pepper ...?!"

* * * * *

Shakir held his arm up as if in a trance. The men saw his lips moving, but they couldn't tell whether he was praying or counting down. Finally, he looked up and pointed at the living room as he spoke into his radio, "Attack!"

* * * * *

Katy, Joshua, and Josh remained poised, each on one knee, in a tight semi-circle, as bullets began zipping into the room from the window.

Joshua cocked his rifle, "They're wearing vests, so aim for their heads."

The first one appeared from the entryway with an AK-47 blazing. His shots slammed into the fireplace. Katy took aim and fired, hitting him in the groin and sending him tumbling to the ground, face-first.

Joshua glanced at her with a grin, "That'll work too."

A rifle poked through the window followed closely by a balaclava-covered head. Young Josh aimed and fired. The head disappeared in an explosion of blood.

A second terrorist appeared from the entryway, at the same time as another leaned in from the window, both letting lead fly.

Katy shot the second one in the thigh, sending him rolling to the ground, while Josh shot the one in the window in the face. He was followed by two others breaking through the window at the same time. Josh and Joshua opened fire at them as four others rushed into the room from the entryway.

With bullets whizzing all around them, Katy, Josh, and Joshua kept firing and cocking, firing and cocking, with Joshua firing the most in every direction. Bodies began piling up on one another in front of the window and entryway.

A bullet smashed into Katy's rifle, ripping it from her hands. Then a bullet slammed into Joshua's thigh, knocking him to the floor.

"Grandpa …!" Josh leaned over his grandfather as Shakir's men overran them and took their rifles away. Shakir's men stood them up, holding them by their arms.

Shakir entered the room from the entryway and pointed to young Josh. His men dragged him over and turned him around to face his mother and grandfather. They pushed him down onto his knees, as one of the men used an electrical cord from a lamp to bind Josh's hands behind his back.

Shakir pulled the familiar serrated, black-handled knife from its scabbard and held it in front of him, "You American pigs … I told you, you would watch me behead your son and grandson …."

Shakir snapped his fingers and one of his men pulled a canister of gasoline out from his pack.

Shakir grabbed Josh by his hair and pulled his head up. Shakir's eyes met Joshua's "I will hand you your grandson's head before I set you on fire."

The sounds of vehicles, followed by men's voices shouting in English came from the window. Everyone's attention in the room turned to one of Shakir's men as he leaned his head out to investigate.

The sound of two automatic-rifle shots rang out in quick succession. The man who had leaned out was knocked straight back onto his feet. He turned to face the room. Blood began pouring from two gunshot wounds to his forehead before he crashed to the floor.

"The American pigs have arrived ... do not allow them to enter the house!" shouted Shakir.

All Shakir's men, except for the one holding the gasoline, ran to the window and front door as a firefight broke out.

* * * * *

"You wanna play with knives?" Joshua's voice got Shakir's attention. Shakir turned to him just in time to see Joshua wind up and throw a twelve-inch *True Flight Thrower* dagger.

The carbon-steel blade pierced through the terrorist's biceps, as young Josh smashed his head into Shakir, knocking them both into the gasoline-wielding fighter. The gas canister fell to the ground next to them.

Joshua caught Katy's eye and nodded to the shattered rifle lying behind her. The bullet from the AK-47 was still lodged in its stock. Wasting no time, she picked it up and tossed it to him.

Josh tried his best, banging his head again and again into Shakir's face, but the enraged terrorist was finally able to get his hands around Josh's throat, subduing him.

The former gasoline-toting fighter got to his feet with rifle in hand just as Joshua locked the trigger on the shattered rifle and used the lever to fire repeatedly. The bullets struck the man in the head and throat killing him before his body dropped back to the floor.

Shakir and Josh were still lying on the floor grappling when Joshua turned and attempted to take aim at Shakir's back, but the turn was too much for his wounded leg. A jolt of pain sent his shot low. The bullet pierced the gas canister. Gasoline began pouring out and puddling under Shakir and Josh, soaking them.

Joshua took aim and fired again. This time the bullet was on target.

Shakir felt the rifle shot strike him on the back of his shoulder. It broke his grip on Josh's throat. Young Josh rolled away gasping for breath.

Shakir got to his feet and turned to face Joshua.

Joshua aimed the rifle between Shakir's eyes and fired. Both men heard the click of the hammer but nothing happened. The rifle was empty.

As the sounds of the firefight continued to rage at the window, Shakir grinned. He took hold of Joshua's blade sticking out of his arm and in one quick motion pulled it out, "I will cut your grandson's head off with your knife."

Joshua took a step to rush forward, but collapsed from the wound to his thigh.

Shakir grabbed young Josh by his hair and lifted him to his knees. He put the knife to his throat …

"Leave my son alone, you ugly son-of-a-whore!" Katy's shout made Shakir turn to face her. His grin disappeared when he realized what she was doing.

Katy lit the cigarette hanging from her lips and took a deep drag. Her eyes locked with Shakir's before she flicked the cigarette at him. Embers flickered in all directions when the cigarette hit the terrorist's boot.

Shakir watched helplessly as the puddle of gas burst into flames. Before he could move, the flames jumped onto his pants and climbed his legs. In seconds he was engulfed in flames. Josh pulled from Shakir's grasp before the flames reached him.

His men at the window ceased firing and turned to watch in horror when they heard his screams, as FBI Agent Shivers rushed into the entryway followed by his men.

For a few gruesome moments, everyone watched as the large ter-rorist leader collapsed to his knees in flames. His screams took on the sound of a wounded animal.

Joshua found his own rifle lying near him. He took aim, and fired. Shakir's body crumbled to the floor looking more like a fire-ball ejected from a volcano crashing to Earth than a human being.

Katy joined Joshua as half the FBI agents rounded up Shakir's men, while the other half did their best to douse the flames. Drop-ping his rifle, he put his arm around her shoulder for support.

She looked at him and allowed a tired smile, "You're right, ciga-rettes will kill ya."

CHAPTER 24

THE DOUBLE-J RANCH
PECOS COUNTY, TEXAS
TWILIGHT

Young Josh helped his mother clean plates away from the long table set up on Joshua's porch. Sitting and standing around the table, drinking and eating, were Freddie and his family, Snake and the Apaches, Angel Martin, and Agent Shivers.

Everyone was listening as Martin recounted how Joshua appeared out of the mist at the hospital, "I'm telling you … Mr. J looked like an avenging angel when he popped out of that fog."

"Where is Mr. J?" asked Shivers.

Katy and Josh looked out toward the pasture.

* * * * *

Joshua stood with a crutch under one arm and his hands tucked into his back pockets. Donning a white, well-worn, felt cowboy hat tilted slightly back on his head, white buttoned shirt with pearl snaps, dust-covered Wranglers, and scuffed boots, he scanned the landscape with dark, deep-set eyes.

The old cowboy nodded with a touch of melancholy, until his gaze was broken by a gentle gust of wind that brought the wind chimes to life perched over Sarah's headstone, behind him. He turned towards the sound.

There, next to Sarah's and James's headstones was Pepper's. He glanced in the direction of the house to see Katy and Josh walking from the hacienda in his direction.

Joshua turned again to Pepper's headstone and saluted it, snapping his arm up quickly before letting it draw away slowly, "Rest in peace, my friend."

He turned to face in the direction of his daughter-in-law and grandson still afar off, but spoke to Sarah, Pepper, and James, "Don't y'all worry ... I'll keep an eye on 'em."

Joshua hobbled over and met them halfway. Katy kissed Joshua's cheek then the three of them walked arm-in-arm together back to the house.

Behind them, the last rays of sunlight reflected off the wind chimes and twinkled onto the three headstones in a rainbow of colors.

###

AUTHOR'S FINAL NOTE
ISIS Is In North Texas, But Didn't Cross the Rio Grande to Get Here
Christian McPhate | June 7, 2016 | 4:30am

Wahib Sadek Hamed claimed to be a terrorist. Shirtless, with tan pants, long beads and shaggy dark hair, the 22-year-old Hamed parked his car in the middle of a roadway in Arlington on May 26, then jumped out of his car and lunged at people who passed in their cars. He then threatened a woman with a knife.

Arlington school resource officer Richard Morrison tased him four times before Hamed fell to the ground, shaking uncontrollably. Police found an arsenal in Hamed's car, including a knife and three loaded weapons, one of them an AK-47, along with 200 rounds of ammunition. "He made some strange remarks about having ties to some type of terrorist group," police told a local news station. The FBI is currently investigating his claims.

Hamed doesn't act like a well-trained terrorist operative, but what the FBI is looking for is any evidence that he had been steered toward violence by a terrorist groups. This is the new frontier of terrorism.

"With the widespread horizontal distribution of social media, terrorists can identify vulnerable individuals of all ages in the United States — spot, assess, recruit, and radicalize — either to travel or to conduct a homeland attack," the agency posted on its website. "The foreign terrorist now has direct access into the United States like never before."

But does that access also include operatives who are slipping across the border? The conflation of border security and counter terrorism is a popular topic, and it comes up often during debates over the southern border of Texas. "The threat poised to Texas by ISIS is very real," Governor Greg Abbot wrote to President Obama in November 2015.

Some of the burden to monitor threats falls on local police. Midland County Sheriff Gary Painter in 2014 claimed he received reports from federal agencies that ISIS operatives are crossing the border with immigrants and drugs. When Congress asked Department of Homeland Security officials about this claim during hearings, they said rumors of this ISIS effort has never been substantiated. John Wagner, an assistant commissioner for the Custom and Border Patrol operations unit, noted that Islamic extremists are much more likely to enter the United States by commercial plane.

Still, the local police are wary. "I think it'd be naive to say that [ISIS is] not here," Painter told a local news outlet this year. "We have found Muslim clothing ... Quran books that are lying on the side of the trail, so we know that there are Muslims that have come across and are being smuggled into the United States."

Finding a discarded Quran and clothing doesn't mean ISIS has crossed the border illegally. But the 69-year-old Painter, who's been serving as the Republican sheriff since 1985, believes the discarded items herald a threat. "It is a major concern and should be a concern to every American that there are openings in the border," he says, "and you can come across anywhere."

His officers, he says, are doing everything they can to stop and check people whom they believe may be here illegally. But finding out if they're ISIS is nearly impossible since "they're not going to come out and tell you that they're ISIS."

Fred Burton, an intelligence expert and vice president of Stratfor, a private intelligence firm, points out that since post September 11, The U.S. has not had an attack from operatives who crossed the Texas border illegally. Attacks committed on U.S. soil were carried out by people who were either citizens or here legally.

Another reason ISIS isn't fond of the border is because it is patrolled and the parts that aren't can be deadly to cross. "There are easier ways to get in," Burton says.

Terrorist-linked attacks in North Texas certainly support the idea that homegrown, "lone wolf" style attacks are a larger threat. Nadir Soofi and Elton Simpson, lived in North Texas when, in early May 2015, they decided to attack a Prophet Muhammad cartoon contest in Garland. Despite wearing body armor and armed with three pistols and three rifles, they were both killed by a Garland police officer but not before they opened fire on the crowd. Simpson, an Illinois native, and Soofi, a Texas native, were carrying 1,500 rounds of ammunition. The investigation showed that Soofi and Simpson had made contact with ISIS through social media sites. They communicated with ISIS through a Twitter account, even going so far as to post about their plan, "'May Allah accept us as mujahideen' #TexasAttack."

The other hallmark of terror-related law enforcement in Texas has been radicalized ISIS supporters trying to leave the United States. The case of Bilal Abood, a 37-year-old Mesquite man born in Iraq, showcases the troubles that can face a would-be terrorist who wants to travel to get involved with ISIS.

In 2013 he tried to board a plane at Dallas-Fort Worth International Airport, claiming he was visiting family, but his real goal was to reach Syria and fight alongside Islamic fighters battling against the Assad regime. A month later he traveled to Mexico, flew to Turkey and eventually made his way to Syria.

When he returned, the FBI paid him a visit and confiscated his laptop. On it, he'd been viewing videos of beheadings and tweeting information about Abu Bakr al-Baghdadi, the leader of ISIS. The

FBI also alleges that Abood swore allegiance to ISIS in June 2014. He did this on Twitter. He confessed to lying to the FBI and received four years in prison.

But the FBI seems to have overlooked Omar Kattan and Talmeezur Rahman, two North Texas college students who allegedly left Texas to fight in the Islamic State's jihad in Syria, according to ISIS' personnel records that NBC news obtained from an ISIS defector in Turkey and reported in May 2016. Kattan graduated with a degree in biology from the University of North Texas in 2011, and Rahman, a native of India, grew up in Kuwait, moved to Frisco and attended Collin College. He's listed in the terrorist files as fighting under the name "Abu Salman al-Hindi." Kattan is believed to be dead.

Burton and other experts caution that the open border could be a threat, just one that has not materialized. It would be easy for ISIS or other foreign agents to enter the United States, if they wanted to take that approach.

In that way, Burton agrees with Painter. "The challenge with the border is trying to identify who these people are and go back and pigeonhole who can potentially be ISIS supporters," he says. "Until we get an ISIS supporter linked to an act of terror to the border, you're not going to get a lot of people in Washington doing anything about it."

The Author

Gerard de Marigny is an American novelist and screenplay writer. Since his 2011 inaugural publication of *THE WATCHMAN OF EPHRAIM (CRIS DE NIRO, Book 1)*, Mr. de Marigny has independently published seven CRIS DE NIRO novels, two ARCHANGEL novellas, and the modern western novella, JOSHUA'S COUNTRY. The CRIS DE NIRO counter-terrorism series is set in the days and years following September 11, 2001 when a non-governmental based counter-terrorism firm is formed to respond to crises born from a variety of modern geopolitical events. The series of books resonate with espionage, sub-genre fiction readers from around the world.

Prior to his writing career, Gerard worked in the financial services industry, and prior to that, he wrote, recorded and produced music for other artists, for television and was a member of the rock band, Americade. He is a graduate of Penn State University. Gerard and his wife Lisa live in the foothills of Las Vegas, Nevada with their four sons, Jared, Ryan, Jordan, and Noah.

Follow Gerard de Marigny

Author's Website: www.GerarddeMarigny.com
Facebook: www.facebook.com/Gerarddem
Twitter: www.twitter.com/GerarddeMarigny
Publisher's Website: www.JarRyJorNoPublishing.com
Contact Gerard de Marigny
mailto:g@GerarddeMarigny.com

Other Titles by Gerard de Marigny

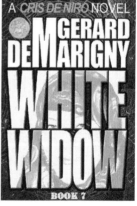

COMING SOON!

THE NEXT INSTALLMENT IN THE JOSHUA'S COUNTRY Series ...

JOSHUA'S COUNTRY:
INVASION

From Master Storyteller
Gerard de Marigny

Made in the USA
Lexington, KY
08 February 2019